PHILIP ALLAN
LITERATURE GUIDE
FOR GCSE

PHILIP ALLAN
LITERATURE GUIDE
FOR GCSE

THE CRUCIBLE
ARTHUR MILLER

Shaun McCarthy
Exam chapters: Jeanette Weatherall
Series editor: Jeanette Weatherall

PHILIP ALLAN
UPDATES

Philip Allan Updates, an imprint of Hodder Education, an Hachette UK company, Market Place, Deddington, Oxfordshire OX15 0SE

Orders

Bookpoint Ltd, 130 Milton Park, Abingdon, Oxfordshire OX14 4SB
tel: 01235 827827
fax: 01235 400401
e-mail: education@bookpoint.co.uk
Lines are open 9.00 a.m.–5.00 p.m., Monday to Saturday, with a 24-hour message answering service. You can also order through the Philip Allan Updates website: www.philipallan.co.uk

© Shaun McCarthy and Jeanette Weatherall 2011
ISBN 978-1-4441-2142-1
First printed 2011

Impression number 5 4 3 2 1
Year 2016 2015 2014 2013 2012 2011

Cover photo reproduced by permission of Andrey Kiselev/Fotolia

Printed in Spain

Hachette UK's policy is to use papers that are natural, renewable and recyclable products and made from wood grown in sustainable forests. The logging and manufacturing processes are xpected to conform to the environmental regulations of the country of origin.

Contents

Getting the most from this book and website

How to use this guide

You may find it useful to read sections of this guide when you need them, rather than reading it from start to finish. For example, you may find it helpful to read the *Plot and structure* section in conjunction with the play or to read the *Context* section before you start reading the play. The sections relating to assessments will be especially useful in the weeks leading up to the exam.

The following features have been used throughout this guide:

● **What are the play's main themes?**

Target your thinking

A list of **introductory questions** to target your thinking is provided at the beginning of each chapter. Look back at these once you have read the chapter and check you have understood each of them before you move on.

Build critical skills

Broaden your thinking about the text by answering the questions in the **Pause for thought** boxes. They are intended to encourage you to consider your own opinions in order to develop your skills of criticism and analysis.

Pause for thought ❚❚

Grade-boosting advice

Pay particular attention to the Grade booster boxes. Students with a firm grasp of these ideas are likely to be aiming for the top grades.

Grade *booster* !

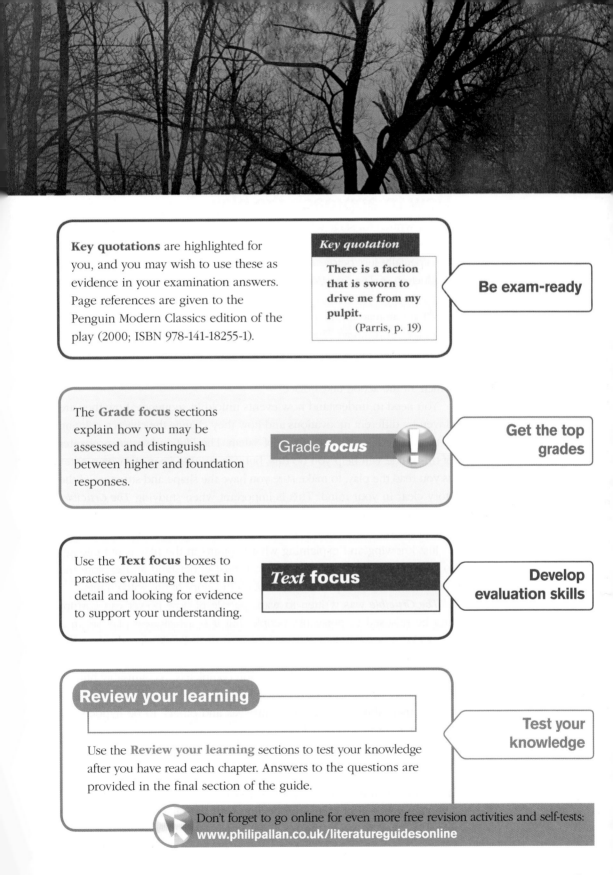

Key quotations are highlighted for you, and you may wish to use these as evidence in your examination answers. Page references are given to the Penguin Modern Classics edition of the play (2000; ISBN 978-141-18255-1).

Key quotation

There is a faction that is sworn to drive me from my pulpit.

(Parris, p. 19)

Be exam-ready

The **Grade focus** sections explain how you may be assessed and distinguish between higher and foundation responses.

Grade *focus*

Get the top grades

Use the **Text focus** boxes to practise evaluating the text in detail and looking for evidence to support your understanding.

Text focus

Develop evaluation skills

Review your learning

Use the **Review your learning** sections to test your knowledge after you have read each chapter. Answers to the questions are provided in the final section of the guide.

Test your knowledge

Don't forget to go online for even more free revision activities and self-tests: **www.philipallan.co.uk/literatureguidesonline**

Introduction

How to approach the play

A play written for stage tells a story through performance. The playwright has to make the audience want to know what is going to happen next — especially just before any break or interval in the performance. In a production of *The Crucible*, the interval usually comes between Acts Two and Three.

What you read on the page will never reveal the full drama and power of a play. As you read *The Crucible*, try to imagine it on a stage: the actors moving about, the scenery around them and the lights changing. Imagine the period clothes and plain rooms in the rough, simple buildings in which all the action takes place.

You need to understand how events unfold in sequence, how they are driven by different motivations and how they change the characters living in the isolated and fearful village of Salem. The *Plot and structure* chapter of this guide will help you do this, but it is good to keep your own notes as you read the play, to make sure you have the shape and structure of the story clear in your mind. This is important when studying *The Crucible*, which has a large cast of characters, many of whom will sound quite similar to you.

Just knowing and explaining what happens in the play is not enough to gain a high mark in an exam. You must understand and explore the themes that Miller is presenting through the story of the witch hunts.

The Crucible was written to warn people of how power can corrupt and be misused to persecute people, but it is a historical play set in a particular time and place that is remote to us today. We need to see the characters in Salem as human beings, different from us in their thinking and understanding of the world, but still completely, recognisably human in the range of things they do: their love for some people and hatred of others, their ability to deceive themselves and others, to be hypocritical or to act according to principles.

Using the text to develop your own ideas

You won't gain a good mark if you just rewrite the ideas in this guide, although you will of course be dealing with the same material from the play. The key to using the text well is to select quotations that really explain points you are trying to make. You need to know the play well in order to know which these are.

You will also gain marks if you can show an understanding of how the text is designed to be used by a theatre company to make a production. Understanding why Miller uses certain stage directions and how these add clarity to what he wants characters to express is important. If you have seen live or recorded productions of the play, you should note things in these that you could use in an answer to show how the story unfolds in a dramatic performance. You might, for example, comment on how the appearance of the characters — all in more or less identical, simple and, to our eyes, dreary clothes — creates a mood of drabness and conformity that reflects the strict moral code of their community.

The girls in the grip of mass hysteria in the Salem court. Why are the girls all dressed alike and what does this uniformity symbolise about their community?

Context

- **How is the play an allegory?**
- **What kind of community was Salem?**
- **How did Miller adapt actual historical events to create a dramatic story?**
- **How did Miller's own experiences motivate him to write the play?**
- **How can we imagine what is added to the text in a stage production?**

An allegorical play

The Crucible is an allegorical play. Miller is dramatising a series of terrible events that occurred in 1692, showing the corruption and hypocrisy that drove people in authority to condemn innocent people to death. He is inviting the audience that he was writing for in the USA in 1953 to see the parallels between what happened in Salem and what was happening in their own country in the 1950s: the investigations of the House Committee on Un-American Activities. (This committee was also confusingly referred to by the acronyms HCUA or sometimes HUAC.)

An allegory is a narrative — in this case, a story based on real events dramatised in a play — that serves as an extended metaphor. It tells one story while constantly inviting us to think about another set of events. While *The Crucible* is a complete theatrical experience based on events that happened in Salem over 300 years ago, it is also a bitter comment by Miller on the work of the House Committee on Un-American Activities.

This committee was charged with seeking out suspected communists living in the USA. Unlike the Salem witch trials, it could not hand down sentences of death, but it could, and did, put people in prison and ruin many others by presenting them — rightly or falsely — as communists to an American public that was fearful and aggressive towards any idea of communism as a potential form of government. Miller was one of many people from the world of arts and entertainment who were brought before the committee, which had a natural suspicion of creative people and artists, many of whom were left wing and socialist, if not out-and-out communists. Miller refused to testify and name others as communists.

The Crucible was Miller's brilliant and stinging response to the work of the House Committee on Un-American Activities. The madness we are plunged into at the start of play is intended to make American audiences in 1953 (when the play opened on stage) see how dangerous and absurd the situation unfolding in Salem appears, then to think that a less violent but no less damaging and absurd witch hunt was happening in their own society. In time, the activities of the committee became commonly known by an increasing group of critics as 'witch hunts'.

The next two sections will give you an overview of the two key areas of background information that you need to understand to see how Miller uses one, the Salem witch trials, to make a forceful attack on the other, the House Committee on Un-American Activities.

The Salem witch trials

Miller based *The Crucible* on actual historical events that took place in Salem, a small puritan community in the province of Massachusetts, in 1692. To make the play work dramatically, Miller altered and rearranged some key events from the actual witch hunts, but all of the main characters are based on real historical figures. The main components of the drama are based on the following historical facts.

A number of young girls, led initially by Betty Parris and Abigail Williams, instigated a series of claims of witchcraft against adults, which were believed by others to be true.

A rather lurid and exaggerated impression of the trials. What atmosphere that is present in the play is the artist trying to capture?

Topfoto

Specially convened courts tried over 150 people on false charges of being witches. All the trials were instigated by an accusation made against a suspect. Nineteen people who were convicted and who refused to confess or name other innocent people were hanged. One man, farmer Giles Corey, was pressed to death under heavy stones. Five people died of illness and ill-treatment in prison.

So many deaths of innocent people, many of whom were previously highly regarded citizens, began to undermine the trials. There were threats of rebellion in some puritan communities in Massachusetts.

The trials were ended in 1693, and over the next 20 years or so the authorities in the province of Massachusetts began to regard them as a grim period of madness. This change of heart is best summed up in a quotation from the real-life Reverend Hale. He wrote a book entitled *A Modest Enquiry into the Nature of Witchcraft* in 1697, though it was not published until 1702. Just like his character in *The Crucible*, Hale was haunted with the guilt of what he had done in Salem. He said of the events that Miller dramatises, 'Such was the darkness of that day, the tortures and lamentations of the afflicted, and the power of the former presidents [the trial judges like Danforth and Hathorne], that we walked in the clouds, and could not see our way.'

However, Miller alters some facts and details to make the play work:

- Abigail was only 11 when the trials took place, but Miller needs to make her a young woman so that she can have an affair with John Proctor and so develop him for the role he has to fulfil in the drama.
- Danforth and Hathorne are not historical figures but are created from what Miller could research about a number of judges involved in the trials.
- Approximately 150 people were arrested, but not all were from the village of Salem. This is the total number of people arrested across the three counties around Salem: Essex, Suffolk and Middlesex — all named after the areas in eastern and southeastern England where the majority of puritans who founded the province of Massachusetts had originally come from.

Pause for thought

In his 'overture' (at the top of p. 14 in the prose passage), Miller suggests that it was the need for constant hard work just to survive that kept many people from breaking the strict puritan guidelines on how to live. Which characters in the play refer to hard work on their farms?

House Committee on Un-American Activities

The work of the committee — broadly to seek out people with political opinions that could be considered a threat to American security — had its roots in investigative committees going back to 1919. The House

Committee on Un-American Activities itself was set up in 1937 and was active throughout the Second World War, investigating 'suspicious' foreign nationals — especially Germans and Japanese, as their home countries were enemy states to the USA during the war.

The committee became especially active after the Second World War, seeking out suspected communists living and working in the USA. The 'Cold War', a long period of mutual suspicion and distrust between the USA, the world's greatest capitalist country, and Russia and its communist satellite states in central and eastern Europe, was just beginning. Many in the USA were terrified of another war and a communist takeover.

In 1947, the committee began an investigation into people working in the Hollywood film industry. A total of 41 people attended the hearing voluntarily. They were known as friendly witnesses. Many accused former friends and work colleagues of having communist sympathies. Then, ten Hollywood film figures, including writers and directors, refused to testify. Each was sentenced to between six months and a year in prison.

As a result of accusations from 'friendly witnesses', over 320 writers and artists were placed on a black list that stopped them from working in the entertainment industry. Miller was on this list, but being blacklisted did not stop his plays being produced in theatres in the USA. Miller was not afraid to say that he supported many things such as workers' unions that many Americans suspected as communist ideas. He also refused to 'name names' and identify anyone he had met at left-wing political meetings in the 1930s. In 1957, he was found guilty of being in contempt of Congress (government) because of his refusal to 'help' the committee. This ruling was overturned a year later, but for many Americans Miller remained a dangerous left-wing radical.

Writing *The Crucible* and having it staged in the USA while the committee was still at work can be seen as Miller's comment — if not his revenge — on them for the way they treated him and others.

Miller wanted *The Crucible* to show clear comparisons between the Salem witch trials and the 'witch hunts' of the House Committee on Un-American Activities. These common features include:

- the narrow-mindedness, excessive zeal and disregard for the individual that characterise a government's or authority's efforts to stamp out a perceived social ill (witchcraft or left-wing communist political opinions)
- encouragement to confess 'crimes' and to 'name names', identifying others who might be witches or sympathetic to their radical cause
- destruction of reputations or 'good names', both by being found guilty in a witch trial or by the committee; and 'by association', by

being named in a trial or before the committee as a friend of an accused or convicted person

One of the most powerful and aggressive figures on the House Committee on Un-American Activities was Senator Joseph McCarthy. He became the public face of the committee's work in the 1950s, to the extent that the term 'McCarthyism' was coined in 1950 to describe any anti-communist hunt or activity. (The author of this guide would like to point out that he is no relation!)

Arthur Miller's political opinions

Miller has been criticised for oversimplifying his comparison between the witch trials and the House Committee on Un-American Activities. There were no actual witches in Salem but there were certainly communists in 1950s America. However, one can argue that Miller's concern in *The Crucible* is not with whether the accused actually are witches, but with the fact that the court officials start the trials unwilling to believe that they are not. This was also true of the investigations of the House Committee on Un-American Activities when it investigated suspected communist sympathisers.

Miller was Jewish, a race that had been persecuted throughout history and almost exterminated in Europe during the Second World War. The Nazis had been murdering Jews in their millions only a few years before Miller began writing the play.

Here are two key quotations by Miller that shed light on his thoughts when he started writing *The Crucible*. The first refers to the situation in the USA when the hunt for communists was on; the second is a broader comment on the abuse of power by a state, influenced by what had happened to the Jews.

> I began to think of writing about the hunt for Reds (communists) in America. I was motivated in some great part by the paralysis that had set in among many liberals who, despite their discomfort with the inquisitors' violations of civil rights, were fearful, and with good reason, of being identified as covert Communists if they should protest too strongly.

> When Gentiles [non-Jews] in Hitler's Germany saw their Jewish neighbours being trucked off…the common reaction, even among those unsympathetic to Nazism, was quite naturally to turn away for fear of being identified with the condemned. As I learned from non-Jewish refugees, however, there was often a despairing pity mixed with 'Well, they must have done something.' The thought that the state has lost its mind and is punishing so many innocent people is intolerable. And so the evidence has to be internally denied.

Setting the scene

Before you begin studying the play, imagine how it opens in stage production. Plays are scripts to be performed by actors. Famous plays like *The Crucible* are usually published, but far, far fewer people sit down and read them than go to see performances. Imagining the play unfolding on stage is vital to understanding how it works and what effects it creates.

The stage lights come up on a bedroom in a simple wooden house. The house is in a small village in a colony that has only been established for around 40 years. The people who founded the colony left Europe because they were persecuted for their extreme religious beliefs and 'pure' lifestyle. Their descendants living in Salem at the time of the play feel completely isolated, geographically and culturally, from Europe. The vast American continent stretches away from the very edges of their farms that surround the village. It is almost completely unexplored, and inhabited by Native American Indians whom the settlers regard as godless heathens. From time to time there is still fighting between the villagers and the Native Americans. Imagine the huge sense of isolation hanging over Salem as you read the play.

Text focus

On p. 16 of his prose overture, Miller says that 'the Salem tragedy' developed from a paradox. A paradox is a statement or group of statements that create a contradiction. It can also define a situation which appears to contradict what we naturally think should be the case. If we apply this idea to the story of the Salem witch trials as Miller dramatises it, we can see how they took place at a point in the development of the puritan colony where some people were beginning to question why such strict rules were needed to control their lives. For some characters in the play, this glimpse of possible new and greater personal freedoms is frightening. Danforth, Hathorne, Parris and the Putnams are fearful of what might happen if greater freedoms are sanctioned. The judges and Parris fear losing authority, while the Putnams may feel unsure about how a more free society would affect their status as major landowners.

There can be nothing in Betty Parris's bedroom, or in the entire colony, that cannot be made by a carpenter, a village blacksmith or by women weaving cloth. There are no sophisticated or 'luxury' items. Adding to this enforced simplicity of the houses is the fact that the puritans hate and ban any form of art or decoration. They dress almost identically in simple black clothes. The stage set needs to convey all this: what the audience sees when the lights first come up is vital to their understanding of the world of the play.

(Answers on p. 87)

Review your learning

1 Why was the American government so fearful of discovering communist sympathisers living in the USA at the time Miller was writing the play (1953)? What parallel was Miller drawing between the government's actions and those of the authorities in Salem?

2 Give two reasons to explain why you think people in Salem became swept up in the hysteria of the witch trials.

3 How do you think the fact that Miller was Jewish and had seen the reports of Hitler's holocaust in the Second World War (1939–45) influenced his desire to write the play?

4 What practical purpose did the rigid conformity of Salem society serve?

More interactive questions and answers online.

Plot and structure

- How does *The Crucible* tell the story of the Salem witch trials in four acts?
- What are the key events of the plot as they occur in sequence through each of the four acts of the play?
- What is the timescale (timeline) of the actions in the play?

Timeline

The Crucible takes place between the spring and fall (autumn) of 1692. The play is constructed in four acts, each of which is really a long scene focusing on one key moment in the unfolding story. Each is set in a different location.

Act	Date	Setting
One	Spring 1692	The upstairs bedroom in Reverend Parris's house
Two	Eight days later	The living room of John Proctor's house
Three	Some weeks later (in summer)	The vestry room of the Salem meeting house (now used as part of the court for the trials)
Four	The fall (autumn)	The jail in Salem

Act One

- Reverend Parris prays beside the bed of Betty, his daughter, who is in some sort of trance. We learn from his niece Abigail and his slave Tituba that Betty, Abigail and other girls have been dancing naked in the woods. Ann and Thomas Putnam arrive and claim that Betty is bewitched.
- Abigail warns the other girls to agree a story to avoid being accused of witchcraft.
- Abigail's affair with John Proctor is revealed.
- Betty cries out, hearing the name Jesus sung in a hymn by people downstairs.
- Rebecca Nurse warns everyone not to be frightened into believing claims of witchcraft.
- Reverend Hale arrives and questions Betty and Abigail and appears suspicious. Abigail stages a denouncement of women whom she claims she has seen with the Devil and the other girls join in.

Betty, the ten-year-old daughter of the Reverend Samuel Parris, lies in bed in her small bedroom. Her father, in his forties, kneels in prayer. Betty is in some kind of trance or fever-induced, semi-conscious state. Parris does not know what to do. He is concerned for his daughter and also afraid, but of what exactly we are not quite sure.

Pause for thought

Susanna quotes Doctor Griggs's suggestion that 'unnatural causes' might be the source of Betty's condition, and Abigail warns Susanna not to speak of this (p. 18). What effect is Miller trying to create by not 'coming straight out' with the possibility of witchcraft as the cause of Betty's condition?

Poster for the film of the play starring Daniel Day-Lewis and Winona Ryder. Which two characters do you think they are playing and what moment in the play might this be?

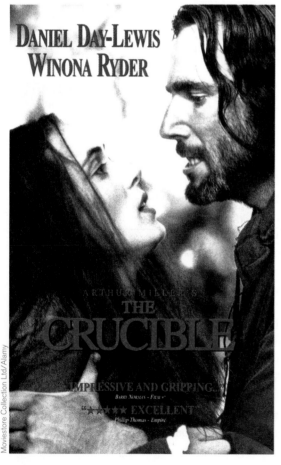

Tituba, Parris's black slave who he brought with him from Barbados, enters. She is concerned for Betty's welfare. She seems a humane and decent woman to have such care for a child who is the daughter of her owner. Parris is angered by Tituba's concern and makes her leave.

Two teenage girls arrive: Abigail Williams, Parris's niece, and Susanna Walcott, who tells Parris that Dr Griggs can find no cure for Betty's ailment. The doctor suggests that unnatural causes may be at work. Abigail warns Susanna not to mention this to anyone. She is angered when her uncle asks her why Goody Proctor won't sit next to her in church.

Key quotation

There is a faction that is sworn to drive me from my pulpit. Do you understand that?

(Parris, p. 19)

Ann Putnam arrives. In most stage plays, the writer gives little or no description of a character at the point where they enter a scene. Miller, however, writes some sharp, dramatic descriptions of characters. Ann Putnam is 'a twisted soul', 'death-ridden', 'haunted by dreams'.

Pause for thought

What does Miller want Ann Putnam's appearance to suggest to us about her character? What kind of role do you think she will play in the unfolding drama?

Ann offers no sympathy to Parris as the father of a sick child, but says, 'It is surely a stroke of hell upon you', as if she is certain the girl is bewitched and that this is some kind of punishment on Parris. She claims that Betty was seen flying 'over Ingersoll's barn'.

Her husband, Thomas Putnam, arrives. He too has no sympathy for Parris and Betty, but seems delighted that 'the thing is out'. He means that the bewitching of girls is now plain to see. He says that their daughter Ruth also has 'the Devil's touch': she is walking about, but as if she is deaf and blind. The Putnams are in no doubt that she is like this because 'Her soul is taken'.

Grade *booster*

In this opening scene, we are plunged directly into a strange and fevered world. To gain good marks you need to be able to explain how this atmosphere is crucial to the impact the play has. People are coming into a bedroom without courtesy or, seemingly, invitation. People take Betty's condition as demonic possession. Stories of girls flying are reported as credible facts. Miller is creating a world where people are twisting situations to suit their own ideas about witchcraft. Miller wants us to see that Salem is an unhealthy and bitter community, where private lives are about to be ripped open for public investigation.

Parris has sent for Reverend Hale of Beverly, another village in the colony, as a 'precaution'. Hale uncovered a witch the previous year.

Parris and Putnam are evenly matched characters in this opening scene. Parris is the spiritual leader of this community; Putnam is the son of the richest man in the village. He has fought off Indian attacks, so has both status and personal bravery to match Parris's spirituality. Parris knows the influence that Putnam wields in the community. There is more than a hint that Parris is afraid of both Putnams' accusations.

Ann Putnam talks of the seven apparently healthy babies she has given birth to, who have died for no clear reason. Ann claims she is a religious woman, yet she appears to have no qualm about using Tituba to try to communicate with spirits. She believes that Tituba can speak to the dead. Ann and her husband believe that there is 'a murdering witch among us'. This pronouncement from such an important figure in the community is full of foreboding. Putnam urges Parris to confess there is witchcraft in the house before he is accused of concealing it. Abigail shows her cunning and deceitful nature: she whispers to her uncle that she did not try to conjure spirits but that Tituba and Ruth did.

Mercy Lewis, the Putnams' servant, arrives to visit Betty. As with Ann Putnam, Miller introduces her with a very unpleasant and sharp description.

Pause for thought

Does Ann's sad story of seven dead children make you feel any sympathy for her? Do you think Miller wants us to feel any?

Pause for thought

There are now five people in the small bedroom. There is a crowd of people waiting for news downstairs. What effect does such a crowded stage convey?

Mercy says Ruth has sneezed, which both she and Ann take as 'a sign of life'. Miller uses the absurdity of this to suggest just how self-deluding and ignorant of health issues these people are.

It is a measure of Parris's loss of control in his own house that when he asks Thomas Putnam to leave so he can pray, the farmer doesn't go until he and Parris go together. Ann Putnam has already gone and so the girls are alone in the bedroom. Mercy discusses Ruth's sickness with Abigail, and suggests beating Betty. Abigail tells Mercy that she has confessed to dancing in the woods, and that she has said that Tituba conjured Ruth's dead sisters, and that Parris saw Mercy naked.

Mary Warren, the Proctors' servant, enters in a panic because the town is talking witchcraft. Abigail shows herself as the most cunning of the girls. When she threatens Betty with a beating, she sits up and cries that Abigail drank blood to kill John Proctor's wife. Abigail 'smashes' Betty across the face.

Key quotation

What'll we do? The village is out. I just come from the farm; the whole country's talkin' witchcraft. They'll be callin' us witches, Abby!

(Mary Warren, p. 25)

Pause for thought

If you were directing the play, what would you tell the actors about Betty's sudden awakening: that she had been feigning sleep all along, or that she was actually in some kind of unconscious state and that Abigail's words have the power to cut through this and wake her? Explain your thinking.

Abigail now takes control, like a ringleader making the gang agree a story to tell. This takes less than two lines of her long speech on pp. 26–27. The remaining eight lines are threats to the others. Miller is letting us know what a bully Abigail is. Betty appears to faint away in fear; Mary is fearful that Betty will die as punishment for conjuring the dead. Abigail turns on Mary, but is cut short by the arrival of John Proctor. He berates Mary for leaving the house, where she is needed for work. Mary goes, and a moment later Mercy 'sidles' out, leaving Abigail alone with Proctor. They both appear to regard Betty as unconscious and behave as if she cannot hear or see them.

Abigail is flirtatious. She speaks tenderly to Proctor and he cannot help but soften his mood a little. We discover that they had an affair when she was the Proctors' servant. Abigail believes that he could be tempted to be her lover again. He kindly but firmly denies it. She claims that he still desires her. The soft mood between them is broken when Abigail is angered by being called 'child' (p. 29).

Key quotation

'I will cut off my hand before I'll ever reach for you again.'

(Proctor, p. 29)

Even John Proctor, whom we come to see as the most reasonable and rational person in the story, readily uses the kind of overheated, extreme and biblically influenced language that is so much a part of conversation in Salem. Instead of saying simply and perhaps more kindly to Abigail that their affair is over, he says he would prefer to mutilate himself than touch her again.

Abigail pleads that she still loves him and insists that he loves her. Downstairs, people are singing a hymn. Hearing the name Jesus sung, Betty sits up and screams. Parris rushes in, followed by the Putnams. Ann Putnam claims that Betty screamed because she could not bear to hear the name Jesus. Parris still refuses to believe that his daughter is bewitched and sends Mercy to bring the doctor.

Text focus

The conversation between John Proctor and Abigail is a good example of how well-written dialogue does three things simultaneously:

● moves the story forward
● develops characters
● delivers back-story and other things that we need to know

Let's see how this works in this scene.

The story is moved forward because John Proctor has made Abigail angry. She appears desperate for his love again. She is capable of being cunning and scheming. Proctor may have made a dangerous enemy of this young girl.

Well-written characters, just like real human beings, are complex. Abigail causes mayhem in this story, yet we can see that maybe she really loves John Proctor and is genuinely hurt by his rejection. Proctor will die for his principles, but these didn't stop him having an affair with his young servant. We don't know if he seduced her or if she seduced him, but either way he broke the rules of his religion. He claims he will never touch her again, but doesn't deny that he 'may have looked' up at her window.

Abigail's speech about Salem's 'pretence' (p. 30) is a key point that Miller wants to make about societies which claim to live by high moral principles: people always fall short of such ideals.

> **Pause for thought**
>
> Abigail is half John Proctor's age. He is married and she was his servant. Do you think Abigail is justified in being angry with him for taking advantage of her, having sex with her, then letting his wife turn her out of her job?

Rebecca Nurse arrives in the bedroom, shortly followed by 83-year-old Giles Corey. Rebecca, who has 11 children and 26 grandchildren, claims that Betty's illness is nothing serious. She is a calm figure, while Giles Corey is old but 'still powerful'. They appear as wise and sensible people and their arrival on stage is intended to contrast with the passion and confusion that has gone before.

Rebecca is sceptical of claims of witchcraft. John Proctor angers Thomas Putnam by saying that he should have called a meeting before sending for Reverend Hale. Putnam accuses

> ### *Key quotation*
>
> **Pray calm yourselves. I have eleven children, and I am twenty-six times a grandma, and I have seen them all through their silly seasons, and when it come on them they will run the Devil bowlegged keeping up with their mischief.**
>
> (Rebecca, p. 32)

Proctor of not attending Sunday church services. Proctor says that Parris preaches only damnation, not the word of God. Rebecca says that people fear to bring their children to church because Parris's sermons are so full of threats of damnation. Parris launches into complaints about his pay and promises made to him in his contract. He appears to have a high opinion of his own worth.

Grade *booster*

A C-grade student would simply explain how this passage (pp. 34–35) shows Parris's greedy side. An A-grade student would relate this to alliances developing between characters. The Putnams seek to extend their property and wealth, so they will at least in part side with Parris. John Proctor, Giles Corey and Rebecca Nurse appear to be concerned less with developing their lands and possessions, and more with asserting reasonable behaviour again.

Rebecca, ever the calm influence, is aware that Proctor may be storing up trouble for himself when he speaks out against Parris. She advises him to make his peace, but Proctor decides to leave. However, he is held back by a discussion between himself, Giles Corey, Putnam and Parris about the number of times disputes in the village involving all these men have ended up in court. Miller includes this to show us that, despite this being a community supposedly bound together by strict religious belief and practice, there are endless legal disputes.

The Reverend John Hale arrives, carrying half a dozen heavy books. He introduces himself to Rebecca Nurse, and says he has heard of her 'great charities' (p. 40). Hale seems keen to be friendly to everyone. Giles, perhaps mischievously, tells Hale that Proctor does not believe in witches. Proctor chooses his words carefully, saying to Hale that he has heard he is a 'sensible' man. Parris agrees to be bound by whatever decision about witchcraft, or the lack of it, that Hale finds.

Pause for thought

Hale is a man who believes he has very thorough knowledge of all the ways the Devil can tempt people. Look up the meaning of 'precise' and explain exactly what you think Hale means when he says (p. 41) 'The Devil is precise'?

Ann Putnam confesses that she sent Ruth to learn from Tituba why all her babies died. We might think she is confessing to this 'crime' as soon as Hale arrives to investigate, rather than waiting for it to be discovered through his investigations. Hale is impressed by this information, suggesting that he sees such misfortune as caused by malign spirits. He consults his books and makes a speech designed to impress the simple farmers about the wisdom they contain.

Grade *booster*

A C-grade student would analyse this scene in terms of what happens to set up the characters in the play. An A-grade student would, in addition, understand how playwrights plant expectations about how events will unfold, then they either fulfil these expectations or surprise the audience by having the plot develop in different ways. In this act, Miller is subtly setting up the two sides for the conflict that will develop.

Hale says he may have to 'rip and tear' to free Betty from the Devil's grip. Rebecca, still a quiet voice of reason, says she is too old for such things and will go. Miller reminds us of the simple nature of the people of this community, when the otherwise sceptical Giles Corey asks Hale if reading 'strange books' might be an evil activity. They are probably strange to him because he is hardly literate. He claims, rather foolishly given the situation, that he finds he cannot pray after his wife has been reading. Hale dismisses his concerns for the moment.

Text focus

Hale's lines on p. 40 — and his description of his books on p. 42 — are designed to show how he uses his specialist knowledge to assume authority over everyone else in the room, including Parris. No one questions his wisdom — although Rebecca is dismissive by her leaving and Proctor observes without real commitment. Much of what Hale says is laughable to us. Most seventeenth-century Christians believed in devils and demonic possession — some Christians still do — but Miller knew that many in his audience would find what Hale says about 'frightful wonders' to be ridiculous. Miller was writing this play largely as an allegory to attack events in the USA in the 1950s. He was inviting his audience to make a connection between the blind faith of Hale and the work of the House Committee on Un-American Activities.

Hale gets no response from Betty when he speaks to her: if she is still play acting, she is very committed to her fantasy. Hale turns threateningly ('*his eyes narrowing*') to Abigail and asks what happened in the forest. Parris claims he saw a kettle, but Abigail says it contained only soup, although a frog may have jumped in it. Hale asks Abigail if she has sold her soul to Lucifer. Abigail blames Tituba, claiming that she made her and Betty drink chicken blood. Abigail says that Tituba sends her spirit on her in church and makes her laugh at prayer. Putnam declares that Tituba must be hanged.

Pause for thought

Miller was a passionate believer in civil rights. What is the significance of Tituba being the first person to be accused and threatened with death?

Tituba on trial. Why has the director placed her in a kneeling position?

Key quotation

I want the light of God, I want the sweet love of Jesus! I danced for the Devil; I saw him; I wrote in his book; I go back to Jesus; I kiss His hand.

(Abigail, p. 49)

Hale confronts Tituba. He asks if the Devil comes to her with anybody else. Tituba admits that the Devil has come to her, promising to return her to Barbados. She claims he has white people working for him, including Goody Good and Goody Osburn. Her confession and naming of others seems obviously driven by panic. Miller is presenting a clear parallel as Act One draws to a close between Hale's crude investigation of Tituba and the many 'confessions' declared to the House Committee on Un-American Activities, when people threatened with ruin named others they said had communist sympathies.

Abigail suddenly claims she must 'go back to Jesus'. She starts a list of accusations against adult women whom she claims are in league with the Devil. Betty rouses from her (real or feigned) unconscious state and joins in. This is a high dramatic point to close the scene. If the scene carried on, Hale would interrogate the two girls and the moment would lose dramatic effect, so the act closes with claims of demonic possession spreading out from the bedroom to touch innocent women around the village.

Act Two

- John and Elizabeth Proctor argue about the affair he had with Abigail.
- There are now active witch trials in Salem. Mary arrives from court. She gives Elizabeth a 'poppet' doll she has made in court to pass the time.
- Hale arrives and questions the Proctors about their knowledge of the scriptures and attendance at church. His visit becomes more

and more like an interrogation. He reveals that Elizabeth has been named as a suspect.

- Ezekiel Cheever arrives with a warrant for Elizabeth's arrest. John Proctor tears it up.
- Giles Corey and Francis Nurse report that their wives have been arrested.
- Elizabeth is taken away. Proctor leads Giles Corey and Francis Nurse in a vow to fight this growing madness.

This act takes place in the Proctors' house eight days later, in what should be considered their private space. Miller uses the setting to develop his theme of the community in Salem constantly and destructively invading each other's private lives. This is most obvious when Hale arrives unannounced, uninvited and startling the Proctors. This is more threatening than if Proctor had gone or been summoned to see Hale in the court or some other public place.

Miller creates an atmosphere of guilt in the Proctor household that mirrors a similar mood throughout this small Puritan society. Elizabeth Proctor cannot forgive her husband for his affair. Miller is suggesting that neither in their household nor in the whole village can people accept that human beings have faults, and sometimes need forgiveness. The Proctors' is not a happy house; neither is the community in Salem.

John Proctor returns from the fields and greets his wife, Elizabeth. There is an awkwardness between them. She thinks he has been to Salem that afternoon, but Proctor says he thought better of it.

Elizabeth tells her husband that their servant Mary Warren is there, and although Elizabeth tried to forbid her from going to Salem, Mary 'frightened all her strength away'. This shows the power the girls are beginning to exert psychologically on adults, even someone like Elizabeth, who in other ways seems a strong-willed woman.

> **Key quotation**
>
> **She frightened all my strength away.**
> (Elizabeth, p. 49)

> **Pause for thought** ⏸
>
> Why do you think Miller writes in the business of John Proctor tasting then seasoning the food? Why would he bother with such a small detail? What might he be suggesting about Proctor?

Miller is showing how the situation in Salem has developed. Mary is now an official of the court, formally accusing people of witchcraft, along with Abigail and other girls. Elizabeth says the whole story is 'a fraud'. She tells John to go to Ezekiel Cheever, who is acting for the court of inquiry, and tell him that Abigail said that Betty's sickness had nothing to do with witchcraft.

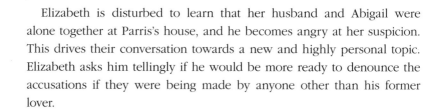

Elizabeth is disturbed to learn that her husband and Abigail were alone together at Parris's house, and he becomes angry at her suspicion. This drives their conversation towards a new and highly personal topic. Elizabeth asks him tellingly if he would be more ready to denounce the accusations if they were being made by anyone other than his former lover.

Grade *focus*

When you write about characters in *The Crucible*, examiners will want to see not only that you know who they are and what they do, but also that you understand how Miller is using key techniques of play writing to develop characters and story simultaneously.

Grade D–G students will use John Proctor's explanation to Elizabeth to explain how he has the problem of keeping his reputation if questioned about how he knows Abigail is lying. This is a personal dilemma about how to act.

Grade A*–C students will explore the principles of play writing that Miller is using here, explaining how playwrights often give a morally good or heroic character a fatal flaw that undermines their better qualities and can finally destroy them. In Proctor's case, this is a sexual affair. A key theme of the play is how this community sought to drag private lives into the public gaze, how everyone felt they had a right to comment on everyone else's business.

Proctor says angrily that he has confessed to his sin; Elizabeth remains cold but claims not to judge him. He replies that her justice would 'freeze beer' (p. 55). We sense that an often-repeated argument is developing. It is stopped by the arrival from court of Mary Warren. John Proctor is angry with her for having left the house and neglected her work. He shakes Mary, but when she complains that she is unwell, he immediately lets her go. Perhaps he is beginning to realise the power the girls have to accuse people who cross them.

Mary gives Elizabeth a poppet, a simple fabric doll that she made in court to pass the time. Mary reports that 39 people have been arrested, and that Goody Osburn will hang, but not Sarah Good because she confessed. Goody Osburn was a poor, elderly beggar who slept in ditches and came to doors, including the Proctors', begging for food and was often turned away hungry.

Grade *booster*

It is good to point out that with Goody Osburn, Miller is letting us see that this community built on strict religious principles is short on charity, one of the three key Christian virtues. It is a further example of a community that is morally rotten.

Mary claims that Goody Osburn sent her spirit out in court to choke them. Proctor demands proof that Goody Osburn is a witch, and forbids Mary to go to court. Mary is amazed that Proctor does not realise the importance of her work. Proctor threatens her with a whip. Mary, reversing the power between servant and employer, says 'I'll not stand whipping any more!' (p. 58).

Text focus

The use of 'any more' in Mary's outburst is a small but significant detail that throws light on Proctor's character. It suggests he has beaten her regularly. It suggests he is a bad employer and a violent man. Perhaps all men in Salem beat their serving girls; perhaps he beat Abigail before he began sleeping with her: but the effect of this detail is to suggest a man who is ready to use violence on young women. Miller is setting up Proctor more and more to be the flawed 'hero' of the story.

Pause for thought

This is the third time since the start of the act that Proctor has lost his temper. What is Miller suggesting about Proctor's character and about the situation he is in?

Mary claims that she saved Elizabeth's life today, for Elizabeth was 'Somewhat mentioned', though not actually accused, in court. Elizabeth realises that Abigail wants her dead. Proctor tells her that he will find Ezekiel Cheever and tell him what Abigail said, but Elizabeth thinks that more than Cheever's help is needed now. She tells her husband to go to Abigail and deny whatever promise he made when they were consumed by passion. Elizabeth shows herself here to be a good judge of character and of the situation. She sees that Abigail is taking a risk by accusing a respected member of society like her. This is more dangerous than accusing an old beggar woman like Goody Osburn. Elizabeth thinks that her husband's blushes of shame when he sees Abigail may be taken as blushes of desire and for the memory of when they made love. John Proctor agrees to confront Abigail: true to character, he is angry again at the thought of what he must do and goes and gets his rifle. He is stopped by the sudden arrival of Hale.

Hale is almost reluctant to reveal why he is calling. His attitude suggests that, in different circumstances, he might feel affinity and kinship with the Proctors. He tells them that Elizabeth's name was mentioned in court and that Rebecca Nurse has now been charged with witchcraft. Proctor finds it impossible to believe that such a good-hearted woman could be in the service of the Devil after 70 years of prayer. Hale reminds him that the Devil is wily and strong.

Grade *booster*

To gain a high mark in the exams, you need to show that you understand how Miller uses what happens on stage to add meaning to the dialogue. Miller writes very detailed stage directions at key moments in the action, as here. Hale appears *'Quite suddenly, as though from the air'*. Miller is suggesting that Elizabeth and John have been so involved in their dispute that they have not noticed him approaching.

Pause for thought

How far do you think that Hale is ready to be driven by his 'knowledge of witchcraft' to accuse even people like the Proctors, that he might usually have respect for? How far might he be speaking 'off the record' here to warn the Proctors of what is happening so that they are not accused unawares?

Key quotation

I cannot think the Devil may own a woman's soul, Mr Hale, when she keeps an upright way, as I have.

(Elizabeth, p. 66)

Hale questions Proctor on his churchgoing habits. He knows — presumably from Parris — that Proctor often misses Sunday services. Proctor says he prays at home and then, perhaps unwisely, criticises Parris for his wasteful spending habits on church ornaments. Hale notes that only two of Proctor's children are baptised. He asks Proctor to state the Ten Commandments. Proctor names nine, but needs Elizabeth to remind him of the tenth — adultery. Proctor says that between the two of them they know all of the Commandments; Hale says that no crack in the fortress of theology can be considered small. The meeting is becoming an interrogation.

Proctor tells Hale how Abigail said Parris discovered the girls sporting in the woods. Hale claims that it is nonsense, as so many have confessed, but Proctor says reasonably that anyone would confess if they would be hanged for denying it! Hale asks Proctor if he will testify in court that there are no witches in Salem, and asks if he believes in witches. Proctor answers that he does not believe that there are witches in Salem, but Elizabeth denies any belief in witches at all. When Hale asks Elizabeth if she questions the Gospel, she retorts that he should question Abigail Williams about the Gospel and not her.

Text focus

The exchanges between Hale and Elizabeth, from her claim that she 'cannot' believe in witches to the arrival of Giles Corey (pp. 66–67) is a good example of Miller showing the harm caused by blurring public life and private convictions. Hale has arrived uninvited, and quizzed the Proctors about their scriptural knowledge and churchgoing habits. He may be doing this to assure himself that they are following the rules of spiritual good conduct. He may want Proctor to help him decide there is no witchcraft in Salem. He may even believe himself to be acting for their benefit, but the meeting becomes an inquisition. When Elizabeth says Hale should question Abigail, she is driven by personal anger towards the girl. This puts her in a bad position when she herself is accused. Miller is showing how no good comes from delving into private lives and dragging out personal secrets. This is exactly what the House Committee on Un-American Activities did every day.

Giles Corey arrives with Francis Nurse to tell the Proctors that their wives have been taken away. Rebecca has been charged with the supernatural murder of Ann Putnam's babies. Hale is troubled by the growing mood of the village. He claims that if Rebecca Nurse is tainted, there is nothing to stop the whole world from burning. He is beginning to see how these accusations could involve everyone. Martha Corey has been taken because of the rumour that Giles stupidly started about his wife reading 'mysterious' books. He is appalled by what he has done.

If there has been a feeling growing that Hale might see reason and side with the Proctors and others who claim that the whole witchcraft claim is false, this is destroyed when he gives his speech on p. 68 to Francis Nurse. He is effectively saying that he might hate what is happening, what he is part of, but he will pursue the accusations on principle. Those who do the bloody work of tyrants have made similar self-deluding and self-justifying speeches throughout history.

Ezekiel Cheever, who is now clerk of the court in Salem, arrives to charge Elizabeth just as Hale has warned and John Proctor has feared. When Giles Corey says to Cheever that he 'will burn' (in Hell) for what he is doing, Cheever says simply that 'I must do as I'm told', then goes on to say he has warrants to arrest 16 people that night. Cheever is repeating the deluded idea of doing one's duty even if that means condoning inhuman acts, just as Hale did earlier.

We begin to realise just how fanatical many people in Salem have become. The village may put its economic survival at risk by slaughtering so many of its own inhabitants rather than shaking off the grip of this madness.

Cheever asks Elizabeth if she keeps any poppets in the house, and she says no. Cheever instantly notices the poppet that Mary Warren made, and finds a needle in it. Cheever recounts the story of Abigail being taken ill over dinner and a needle being found sticking into her stomach. Abigail has testified that Elizabeth's spirit pushed the needle into her.

Mary Warren enters and tells them how the poppet got into the house, and claims that she stuck the needle in it just to keep it safe, but Hale questions whether or not her memory is accurate or supernatural.

Elizabeth calls Abigail a murderer who must be ripped out of the world. Miller needs to raise the dramatic tension of the act as it draws to a close (especially as in most productions there will now be an interval before Act Three). The conflict is increased by Proctor ripping up the

Pause for thought

Can you think of — or find through research — any times in history when people have made the same claim as Hale when pursing a violent and bloody courses of action against innocent people?

Grade *booster*

You must be able explain how the play is constructed to gain an A*–C-grade mark. Each act is one long scene set in a particular room. These are broken up mainly by the arrival or exiting of different characters. In Act Two, the private space of the Proctors' house fills with outsiders and the power that the Proctors have over events is reduced.

Pause for thought

Why do you think Cheever asks about poppets as soon as he arrives? How do you think the needle came to be in Abigail's stomach?

Pause for thought

Mary appears very frightened and hesitant when questioned by Hale about the needle. Do you think she is genuinely frightened about the trouble she has innocently caused or is conspiring with Abigail?

Key quotation

> I'll tell you what's walking Salem — vengeance is walking Salem. We are what we always were in Salem, but now the little crazy children are jangling the keys of the kingdom, and common vengeance writes the law!
>
> (Proctor, p. 72)

warrant Cheever has for Elizabeth's arrest. He calls Hale 'a broken minister'. He says that he will not give his wife to vengeance. This is coming close to confessing that Abigail has a reason for wanting vengeance on both the Proctors, but such is the emotional pitch of the moment that no one questions exactly what John Proctor means.

Cheever takes Elizabeth away. Giles sides with Proctor against Hale. Hale tries to mediate with the angry men whose wives have been arrested. He underlines the madness of the situation when he says 'The jails are packed…and hangin's promised.'

Text focus

Hale says 'hangin's promised' — not 'possible' or 'regrettable', but 'promised'. It is as if he knows the general madness in Salem will not be satisfied until people are executed. He tries to suggest that there is some kind of middle ground. He won't say that the whole thing is a fraud, but neither does he say that all is justified. He claims somewhat vaguely that the court should look to 'cause proportionate' (p. 73). It is not clear exactly what he means, as this is not a legal term in any sense we would understand, but he seems to be suggesting that the Devil may be targeting Salem because serious crimes such as murder and blasphemy have been committed in the past and the guilty parties never punished.

Hale goes. Proctor, Giles and Francis Nurse appear defeated. Proctor demands that Mary Warren come to court with him and tell them that all the witchcraft accusations are false. She warns Proctor that Abigail will charge him with lechery, but Proctor insists that his wife shall not die for him. Proctor again shows his violent side: when Mary Warren sobs that the others will turn on her, he grabs her by the throat.

Danforth surrounded by other judges from the court. What impression of the judges is this still from a film version of the play trying to convey?

Act Three

- Mary Corey defends herself against accusations of being a witch made by the Putnams. Giles Corey claims that the Putnams are making false claims to gain land.
- Francis Nurse claims that the girls' testimonies are all false.
- John Proctor brings Mary Warren to court.
- Proctor submits a document signed by 91 citizens testifying to the good names of condemned women.
- Corey is arrested because he won't reveal a witness to support his claim that the Putnams' daughter is crying false witness.
- Hale, beginning to doubt the truth of the accusations, urges Danforth to listen to Mary Warren's deposition. Danforth questions her.
- Cheever brings Abigail and other girls in from the court. Hathorne suggests that Mary Warren pretend to faint as she had done before, but she claims she cannot do it now.
- Proctor admits his affair with Abigail. Danforth orders Parris to fetch Elizabeth. If she admits to knowing about the affair, Danforth will charge Abigail. Proctor says his wife would never lie.
- Elizabeth is questioned with her back towards Proctor so they cannot communicate. Trying to protect his reputation, she says her husband never had an affair.
- Abigail, then the other girls, pretend to see demons and visions. Mary Warren begs the adults to see that the girls are lying.
- Abigail accuses Proctor of being the Devil's man.
- Hale quits the court in disgust.

This act is one long scene with many characters coming, or being brought, to see the judges. It is important to see events as a dramatic sweep that shows how everyone in Salem has been drawn into the witch trials: as victims, eager or appalled witnesses, judges and officials. The act presents us with a community where normal life is suspended. Miller wants us to follow the main story of John and Elizabeth Proctor and see, through the stories of minor characters, that Salem is tearing itself apart in a kind of self-hatred.

Text focus

The first lines of the act are a seemingly simple exchange:

HATHORNE'S VOICE: Now Martha Corey, there is abundant evidence in our hands to show that you have given yourself to the reading of fortunes. Do you deny it?

MARTHA COREY'S VOICE: I am innocent to a witch. I know not what a witch is.

HATHORNE'S VOICE: How do you know, then, that you are not a witch?

Miller is presenting us with an example of the kind of twisted logic that confused many simple women in Salem into confessing things that were untrue. It is the sort of reasoning that is used to trap people, not to discover the truth.

The act opens in an unusual way, with the stage empty and voices speaking in the next room. Judge Hathorne is questioning Martha Corey.

From outside the building. Giles Corey shouts that Thomas Putnam is reaching out for land. Danforth, the Deputy Governor, silences him. Corey forces his way into the court with Hale. Corey presents himself to Danforth and Hathorne, but it is clear, to him at least, that the Putnams are accusing his wife of witchcraft only because they are trying to destroy his family and take his land. Corey says he means no disrespect to the court, but he is distraught at the harm he has caused his wife by saying (in Act One) that she read 'mysterious' books.

Francis Nurse tells Danforth he has proof that the girls are frauds. He is referring to Mary Warren coming to court to support this claim.

Danforth reminds Nurse — and lets us know — that he now has 400 persons in jail, with 72 condemned to hang. Francis defers to Danforth's position and status, but nonetheless tells him he is deceived. Miller is setting up a public arena where the innocent are forced to deny guilt. In the courts of most democratic countries, it is the other way round: you are presumed innocent until proved guilty. It is into this unfair court that John Proctor now enters.

Parris warns Danforth that Proctor 'is mischief'. Proctor tells Danforth that Mary Warren has signed a deposition that she never saw any spirits, and he tries to present this. Parris thinks that they have come to overthrow the court.

Text focus

Almost the first question Danforth asks Proctor is 'have you given out this story in the village?'. It seems a strange question to ask when we think Salem is totally under the command of those who want witches sought out and judged. In fact, we come to learn later in the play that in another village people rebelled when accusations of witchcraft started to involve more and more people. Danforth is presented as the most intelligent and capable of the judges and it may be that he is weighing up the chance of rebellion in Salem if a man like Proctor (and others) support a deposition that could destroy the basis of the whole witch hunt.

Mary admits that her fits of bewitchment were pretence. Danforth asks Proctor if he intends to undermine the court. Cheever tells Danforth how Proctor ripped up the warrant and that Proctor ploughs his fields on Sundays instead of attending church. Proctor asks Danforth if it strikes him as odd that the accused women have lived so long with such an upright reputation, only to be accused.

Danforth says he has 'seen marvels in this court'. In fact, he has seen teenage girls play acting, carried away by the trouble they have caused. Sophisticated in terms of the world of Salem he may be, yet he decides at this point to believe their acting is demonic possession.

Danforth tells Proctor that his wife is pregnant. Proctor did not know this, but says that Elizabeth never lies. Danforth agrees to let Elizabeth live another month so that she may show signs of pregnancy, and if she is pregnant she will live another year so that she may deliver.

> **Pause for thought**
>
> Why might Danforth, the most senior representative of authority in the play, be so ready to believe the presence of witchcraft? What motives might he have for encouraging the trials to expand to involve more and more people as accusers and victims? Can you link his motives to those of the prosecutors of the House Committee on Un-American Activities?

Text **focus**

Making Elizabeth pregnant is a powerful dramatic device that Miller uses to show the cruelty and madness that has infected this religious community: that they will let a woman bear a child, then kill her and make the child motherless. After the hangings in Salem, there were many orphans who struggled to survive.

Proctor submits a deposition to Danforth signed by 91 citizens, attesting to their good opinion of Rebecca, Martha Corey and Elizabeth Proctor. Parris demands that these 91 be summoned for questioning, and claims it is an attack on the court. When Hale asks if every defence is automatically an attack on the court, Parris says that all innocent and Christian people are satisfied with the courts. Hathorne reads the deposition, and asks which lawyer 'drew' (wrote) it: Giles says that he did. Hathorne is amazed that an elderly farmer could do this, but Giles says he has been a plaintiff in 33 court cases, so has great experience with the law. Hathorne's father even tried a case of Corey's.

> **Pause for thought**
>
> What is the mention of Giles Corey's involvement in 33 court cases intended to make the audience think?

Corey claims that the Putnams are accusing people in order to buy their lands after they have been found guilty and executed. Urged to reveal who heard Thomas Putnam planning this, Corey refuses to reveal his source. Corey is fearful of becoming enmeshed in the court's twisted logic; he sees that the judges seem disposed to believe all accusations of witchcraft over possible logical reasons for these accusations. This new turn in proceedings further shows how divided and bitter the community in Salem has become.

Thomas Putnam arrives and is told that there is an accusation that he prompted his daughter to cry 'witchery' upon George Jacobs. Giles claims that the proof is that, if Jacobs hangs for a witch, he forfeits his property and only Putnam can buy it. Giles claims that someone told him that he

> *Key quotation*
>
> **The proof is there! I have it from an honest man who heard Putnam say it! The day his daughter cried out on Jacobs, he said she'd given him a fair gift of land.**
>
> (Giles, p. 87)

heard Putnam say that his daughter gave him a fair gift of land when she accused Jacobs. Giles refuses to name this person, however. Danforth threatens Giles with contempt: Giles responds that this is not an official court session. Danforth instantly states that the court is now in session and arrests Giles for contempt. Hale (p. 88) sounds a note of caution, saying that the court is increasingly feared.

Giles makes a rush for Putnam, but Proctor holds him back. Proctor and Giles appear to bond together to force the court to act justly. Mary Warren is in tears. Proctor comforts her and begins to present the girl's deposition. Hale advises Danforth that what Mary has confessed could be the truth, and Danforth agrees, 'with deep misgivings'.

Hale is now cast in the role of the henchman who has a growing sense of guilt and conscience: he has signed 72 death warrants, the latest on Rebecca Nurse, and he says that his hand still shakes from doing it. He urges Danforth to agree to lawyers taking on and presenting Mary's deposition.

Pause for thought

Why does Danforth have such misgivings?

Grade *booster*

Miller keeps us engaged with the action in the long scenes by constantly playing with our expectations of how things will develop. Here we see two of the most powerful men conducting the trials shaken by the potential impact of Mary Warren's deposition. Miller wants us to think and hope that common sense will prevail and the trials and executions will be stopped.

Text focus

Danforth's speech on p. 90 is an example of how the prosecutors in the trials used twisted logic to ensure the accused did not have a fair hearing. Danforth argues that using witchcraft is an 'invisible' crime: the witch will not confess, so the only admissible evidence can be from the victims. That is more or less the same as saying that the court will only listen to one side of every argument. Furthermore, the court is 'most eager for all their confessions', so it is keen to find witches rather than keep an open mind and search for the truth.

Parris wishes to question the children accused of false accusations, but Danforth refuses. He questions Mary, who claims that she is with God now (because she has renounced the Devil). Danforth tells her that she is either lying now or was lying earlier, and in either case has committed perjury. This is another example of the twisted logic that traps and condemns, but never explains or illuminates.

Cheever brings Abigail and some of the other girls in from the adjacent court. Abigail tells Danforth that Goody Proctor always kept poppets. Proctor claims that he believes Abigail means to murder his wife, and orders Mary to tell Danforth how the girls danced in the woods naked. Parris tells Danforth that he never found anybody naked, but admits to finding them dancing. Hathorne suggests that Mary Warren should pretend to faint as she had done before, but she claims she cannot do it now. She once thought she saw spirits, but now she does not. Her speech at the top of p. 96 is a clear confession that she cried spirits with the other girls in a kind of group hysteria.

Danforth demands that Abigail search her heart and tell the truth, but instead of being fearful of the powerful judge, she threatens him with the idea that the powers of Hell may turn his wits. Abigail then — suddenly and far too conveniently — pretends that she feels a sharp wind threatening her. She is acting out the visions of demons and other signs of witchcraft we have heard so much about, but until now have not seen. Mercy Lewis then Susanna Walcott join in. Danforth appears ready to consider the idea that Mary Warren is trying to 'witch' Abigail.

Proctor calls Abigail a whore, grabs her by the hair and finally confesses his affair with Abigail. He is distraught at having to destroy his good name but desperate to have his wife seen as an innocent victim of Abigail's jealousy and cunning. He claims that Abigail wants to 'dance with me on my wife's grave'. Everyone realises that if this is true, it provides a clear motivation for Abigail lying and wanting Elizabeth Proctor dead. They see that Elizabeth must know of the affair; that is why she sacked Abigail.

Danforth orders Parris to fetch Elizabeth. If she admits to knowing about the affair, Danforth will charge Abigail. Proctor says his wife would never, could never lie, even to save his name.

Elizabeth is questioned with her back towards Proctor so they cannot communicate. She claims that she sent Abigail away because she displeased her, and because she thought that her husband might be tempted by her beauty. She is adamant that he never committed lechery. Proctor cries out for Elizabeth to tell the truth, that he has already confessed, but Danforth orders Elizabeth to leave.

Proctor says Elizabeth wanted to save his reputation. Hale claims that it is a natural lie to tell, and to stop the trials before another innocent person is condemned.

Pause for thought

Why is Parris so keen to keep the claims of witchcraft alive?

Grade *booster*

To gain a good mark in an examination, you should be able to imagine the play performed and say how Miller's detailed directions for actions create dramatic moments. Here, young girls on the verge of being shown to be frauds utterly take control from serious, senior judges, sweeping away their authority with hysterical play acting.

As in all the acts, the dramatic tension mounts to a climax in the last moments. Hale finally states what he has edged towards throughout this act: that Proctor is telling the truth that the girls have lied. Abigail, in a desperate bid to stop this idea developing, suddenly *'with a weird, wild, chilling cry'* claims that she sees Mary Warren's spirit manifested as a bird, trying to hurt her. Susanna joins in, while Mary Warren begs the adults to see that the girls are lying. Abigail refuses to stop her charade; Mary submits and accuses Proctor of being the Devil's man. She says that Proctor made her sign the Devil's book and made her try to overthrow the court. Danforth orders Proctor to admit his allegiance with Satan. Proctor cries out that God is dead, and that a fire is burning because the court is 'pulling Heaven down and raising up a whore'. Hale denounces the proceedings and quits the court. The act ends in a riot of falsehoods, fury and division. Salem is tearing itself apart.

An artist's impression of events towards the end of Act Three. What mood is the picture trying to capture and convey?

Act Four

- Danforth and Hathorne arrive in the filthy jail where Sarah Good and Tituba are guarded by a drunken Herrick.
- Hale is comforting many condemned prisoners in the jail. Parris says that Abigail and Mercy Lewis have vanished, taking his savings.
- Rebecca Nurse is due to be hanged if she doesn't confess witchcraft. John Proctor is also due to hang this day. Danforth refuses to halt the executions.
- Elizabeth and John Proctor meet. John ask his wife what she would think if he confessed to false allegations to escape hanging. Rebecca Nurse enters and is shocked that John would even consider such a course of action.
- Danforth insists that John Proctor signs a written confession and denounces others. He refuses and he goes with Rebecca Nurse to be hanged.

Act Four takes place in Salem jail cell in the autumn, where condemned women are kept in rags. Sarah Good and Tituba have clearly endured bad

Topfoto

conditions. Tituba seems to be deranged by what she has suffered: she says they will be going to Barbados as soon as the Devil arrives to fly them away.

Hopkins, a guard, announces that the Deputy Governor Danforth has arrived. The women are hauled out and some attempt is made — perhaps out of guilt — to tidy the filthy cell.

Key quotation

Oh, it be no Hell in Barbados. Devil, him be pleasure-man in Barbados, him be singin' and dancin' in Barbados.

(Tituba, p. 108)

Pause for thought

What impression of the jail, its conditions and its 'staff' is Miller wanting us to gain from the opening of Act Four?

Danforth enters with Hathorne. We learn what has happened in the few months that have passed since the end of Act Three. Hale has returned and is going among the condemned prisoners to pray with them. Parris is with him, and the two men are currently visiting the jail. Hathorne wonders if it is wise to allow the increasingly deranged-looking Parris to spend time with prisoners. Cheever talks of cows wandering the streets, untended now that their masters are in jail. He says Parris spent the previous day arguing with farmers about who owned which cattle. This reminds us that Salem is a place of constant mean disputes.

Parris enters, *'gaunt, frightened and sweating'*: a changed man. He says that Hale has been begging Rebecca Nurse to admit to witchcraft to avoid being hanged.

Pause for thought

What do you think has brought about this change in Parris?

Parris says that Abigail and Mercy Lewis have vanished, taking his strongbox of money. He is penniless. He says there are rumours of a rebellion against witchcraft trials in Andover, another settlement in the province.

Hathorne claims that all have been happy with the Salem executions. Parris says that Rebecca Nurse and John Proctor are respected members of the community: their executions will stir up discontent. Parris suggests postponing the executions, claiming that there is dissatisfaction with the courts in Salem now, as shown by the low turnout at Proctor's excommunication. Parris fears for his safety, having found a dagger at his doorway.

Key quotation

Now hear me, and beguile yourselves no more. I will not receive a single plea for pardon or postponement. Them that will not confess will hang...and the village expects to see them die this morning.

(Danforth, p. 113)

Grade booster

You will gain marks for showing how Miller was writing an allegory, inviting us to think about all regimes that abuse power and pervert principles. Salem is split, damaged and divided, yet the judges insist on pressing forward with executions as if they dare not stop. This clinging to power, conducting executions up to the last minute of a failing authority, happens in many unjust regimes that refuse to see reason.

Danforth refuses to halt the executions. Hale paints a picture of Salem (p. 114) with rotting crops and everyone afraid of being denounced.

Danforth summons Elizabeth Proctor but asks Hale to speak to her. Danforth is clinging to what he misguidedly thinks of as his duty. He is still ready to see innocent people die.

Hale tells Elizabeth he will consider himself a murderer if her husband hangs. He says that God damns a liar less than a person who throws their life away. Danforth wonders if there is any wifely tenderness in Elizabeth. Elizabeth asks to speak with her husband. John Proctor shows signs of being tortured. Their meeting is full of love and tenderness, contrasting with the perverse, heartless world they are caught in.

The notice board that stands at the Salem cemetery or 'burying point'. The sign was put up many years after the witch trials: why do you think Hathorne might have objected if he had been alive?

John Proctor asks about their unborn child and their boys. Elizabeth tells him that Giles Corey is dead; he would not answer to his indictment and the court pressed him to death by laying stones on his chest. He died rather than confess anything. Proctor asks Elizabeth what she would think if he confessed. He says he is tempted. She says that she cannot judge him, he must do what he wishes, but she does want him alive. Elizabeth blames herself for forcing her husband to turn to lechery. Proctor tells Hathorne that he will confess to the false charge, but asks Elizabeth once again if it is evil. She says again she cannot judge. When the judges demand a written confession, Proctor is shocked. Danforth says it is for the good instruction of the village.

THE BURYING POINT
1637
Oldest Burying Ground in the City
HERE ARE BURIED
• CAPT. RICHARD MORE
  MAYFLOWER PASSENGER
GOV. SIMON BRADSTREET
REV. JOHN HIGGINSON
CHIEF JUSTICE BENJAMIN LYNDE
JUSTICE JOHN HATHORNE
of the Witchcraft Court

The guards bring in Rebecca Nurse, who is astonished that John is considering confessing. Danforth demands that Proctor prove the purity of his soul by accusing others. This is too much falsehood for Proctor and he refuses. Hale, trying to save Proctor, urges that it is enough that Proctor confess himself. Parris agrees, but Danforth once again demands that Proctor sign the document. Proctor says that he has confessed to God, and that is enough. He asks how he can teach his children to walk like men when he has sold his friends. He wishes to keep only his name.

Pause for thought

What exactly do you think Proctor means by 'keeping his name'? What is he referring to that is so important to him?

Travstock/Alamy

Danforth refuses to accept his unsigned confession and orders Proctor to be hanged. Rebecca and Proctor are led away to the gallows. Hale is desperate to stop this final perversion of justice and waste of innocent lives. He begs Elizabeth to go and plead with Proctor, but Elizabeth says, 'He have his goodness now. God forbid I take it from him!' A drum roll from off stage indicates that Rebecca and Proctor have been hanged.

Review your learning

(Answers on p. 87)

1 Write one word or a short phrase to describe as neatly as you can the key characteristics of the following people, as far as we meet them in Act One:
- Parris
- Abigail
- Ann Putnam
- Thomas Putnam
- Hale

2 What unites Giles Corey, Francis Nurse and John Proctor at the end of Act Two? What is different for each of them in their quest for justice?

3 Miller sets up several moments in Act Three when we think Danforth might come to see that the witch hunt is based on lies. Identify these. Say what happens that allows the trials to continue.

4 Explain the very different reasons for why Hale and Parris are so changed and distressed when they reappear in Act Four.

More interactive questions and answers online.

Characterisation

- Who are the characters?
- How do they relate to one another?
- What does each character want? (What is their motivation for acting as they do in the story?)
- Do they get what they want?
- What stops them getting what they want or opposes their wishes?
- What evidence can we find in the play to help us understand and write about each character?

Characterisation and themes

In a well-written play like *The Crucible,* all the elements that make it work — plot, style of writing, characterisation and themes — are moulded together. Understanding how particular characters are used to develop themes will help you make sense of the play — and gain you higher marks. You could develop your understanding by starting with these 'thumbnail sketches' of how the actions of key characters link to specific themes.

Themes explored	In the actions and roles of
Authority and dissent	Danforth and Hathorne (authority figures who sit in judgement)
Intolerance	Hale and Parris (have no tolerance for those who have opinions different from theirs)
	Danforth and Hathorne (intolerant of individuals who dissent from the court's laws)
Hysteria	Abigail, Susanna Walcott, Mercy Lewis, Mary Warren
Reputation	John Proctor (in a positive way)
	Parris (in a negative way)
Gaining empowerment	Parris and Hale (gaining spiritual authority)
	Ann and Thomas Putnam (gaining material power)
	John and Elizabeth Proctor (gaining personal moral empowerment)
	Abigail and the other girls
Accusation and confession	Abigail and the other girls
	Ann and Thomas Putnam

Themes explored	In the actions and roles of
Sin and guilt	John and Elizabeth Proctor
	Hale
Self-interest	Parris
	Danforth and Hathorne
	Abigail and the other girls
	Ann and Thomas Putnam

Characters in an allegorical play

The Crucible is an allegorical play and the characters are not written to be entirely natural. The large cast play key but often quite simple roles in the story. Some, John Proctor and Reverend Hale especially, are quite complex characters. They have contradictory elements to their personalities and undergo significant changes in what they think and feel as the story unfolds. Crucially, they face serious moral dilemmas and are changed by their actions.

Other characters, such as Parris and the land-grabbing farmer Thomas Putnam, are very simply drawn by Miller. They don't have any of the complexities of real human beings. The play has so many characters that it would be impossible for Miller to make them all fully detailed like real human beings, or like characters in plays with smaller casts.

> ### Grade *booster*
>
> Showing knowledge of other works by the playwright will help you gain marks in the examination. You might compare the detail and conflicting thoughts and emotions that Miller gives the main character in another of his plays: Eddie Carbone in *A View from the Bridge*. The action of this play is entirely built around Eddie's character, while *The Crucible* is about a large number of characters all caught up in a dark period of American history.

There are 21 characters in the play. In order to grasp what role they each play, it is useful to divide the cast into three groups and plan your study of characters according to how important they are.

Main characters are central to the story of the play and are to some extent developed to have conflicting feelings and motives, and to face moral and spiritual dilemmas. For example, John Proctor wants to live and be with his family, but he will not betray his principles and sign a false confession in order to save himself.

Supporting characters have similar conflicting motivations and also face dilemmas, but these are explored with less depth and have less impact on the play than those of the main characters. For example, Danforth is aware that he may be convicting women on false testimonies, but he is driven to continue in order to avoid admitting that any of his

past actions have been wrong. We do not see Danforth wrestle with his conscience over this conflict, as Hale (a main character) does with his role in the witch trials. Danforth also only has any input into the play in two of the four acts, which underlines his status as a supporting character.

Minor characters have smaller parts to play in the drama. Miller does not reveal them to us as fully three dimensional, though they still appear motivated by the very human drives and frailties that appear elsewhere in the play.

Main characters	Supporting characters	Minor characters
John Proctor	Thomas Putnam	Betty Parris
Elizabeth Proctor	Ann Putnam	Tituba
Reverend Samuel Parris	Rebecca Nurse	Mercy Lewis
Reverend John Hale	Mary Warren	Susanna Walcott
Abigail Williams	Giles Corey	Francis Nurse
	Judge Hathorne	Marshall Herrick
	Deputy Governor Danforth	Hopkins
	Ezekiel Cheever	Sarah Good

Note that in the Penguin edition on which this guide is based, Herrick is not listed in the first cast list at the start of the play, where the names of actors playing each character in the 1954 Bristol Old Vic production are given. He is in the list of characters on the next page. This may be because Herrick's small part was cut from the Bristol Old Vic production of the play.

Main characters

John Proctor

John Proctor is the voice of reason and justice in the play. He is the most complex character. He has the intelligence and integrity to recognise and address clear moral dilemmas, yet he is also a flawed human being. He is quick to anger and had a sexual affair with Abigail when she was his servant.

John Proctor has some of the darkest and most passionate speeches in the play. On p. 74 he uses vivid and violent images reminiscent of the Bible's Old Testament stories to terrify Mary Warren, when he accompanies his attack on her at the end of Act Two with the line 'I will bring your guts into your mouth but that goodness will not die for me!' You can use this quotation as evidence of:

- Proctor's violent nature
- his desperate love for his wife
- Miller's construction of a style of language that was based on the King James Bible

Proctor leads the attempts to expose the girls as frauds, but he does not do this until his wife is imprisoned. He does not pursue what we are intended to see as a just and sensible course of action out of public duty, but for personal ends. This element of his character is developed at the end of the play when he is — for a while — prepared to sign a false declaration to save himself.

Despite this understandably pragmatic and sometimes self-interested approach to the problems that confront him, John Proctor finally shows himself to have stronger moral principles than anyone else in the play — with the exception of Rebecca Nurse. Danforth pushes him to sign a written confession and to denounce others — others whom Proctor knows are innocent. Although Proctor wants desperately to live and see his family grow, this is a moral compromise too far and he dies for his principles.

John Proctor is the tragic hero of the play, not just because he is executed by an unjust system, but because, in the tradition of classic heroes, he has a fatal character flaw or weakness that directly contributes to his death. He has a sexual affair with his serving girl, Abigail, while claiming to be a good member of a strict puritan community. He is both an unfaithful husband and a hypocrite, although his disengagement from the community (avoiding church, rarely leaving the farm) suggests that he is full of guilt for his actions. Abigail was his servant and is less than half his age, so we may think that he led the seduction as the more powerful figure. However, Abigail shows herself able to attempt to seduce him when they are alone together in Betty Parris's bedroom, so perhaps she seduced him before. Miller does not make clear whether John Proctor is a predatory seducer or merely a weak man who gave in

> **Key quotation**
>
> **I will bring your guts into your mouth but that goodness will not die for me!**
> (Proctor, p. 74)

> **Key quotation**
>
> **Because it is my name! Because I cannot have another in my life. Because I lie and sign myself to lies! Because I am not worth the dust on the feet of them that hang!**
> (Proctor, p. 124)

Pause for thought

Do you think John Proctor is a religious man? How far do you think he is motivated by Christian principles?

Pause for thought

On a scale from 1 to 10, with 10 as 'very bad' and 1 as 'weak but basically good', where do you think Miller wants us to base our opinion of John Proctor? Give reasons from your reading of the play to support your rating.

to sexual temptation. He is shown to have a strong temper that gets the better of him on several occasions.

Within the limits of his small farming community, Proctor is an intelligent man who can detect foolishness, self-interest and self-deception in others and be ready to expose it. He is able to question his own moral sense.

Elizabeth Proctor

Elizabeth shares with her husband a strict adherence to justice and moral principles. She is a woman who has — at least when we first meet her in Act Two — great confidence in her own morality and in the ability of a person to maintain a sense of righteousness, both internal and external, even when this principle conflicts with strict Christian doctrine. She is a harsh and unforgiving judge of her husband's affair with Abigail.

John and Elizabeth Proctor in a scene from a film version of the play, played by Daniel Day-Lewis and Joan Allen. Which moment from the play do you think this is?

Text **focus**

When John comes home from the fields to Elizabeth at the start of Act Two, he repeatedly comments upon her harsh and unforgiving nature. Although it seems fair to us that she should be angry at her husband's affair with Abigail, the power of John Proctor's repeated complaints about his wife's lack of forgiveness does make us wonder if she is too harsh. You can build a vivid picture of this dynamic between them by using all or some of the following quotations (all spoken by John Proctor):

'You forget nothin' and you forgive nothin'.' (p. 55)

'…and still an everlasting funeral marches round your heart' (p. 55)

'Let you look sometimes for the goodness in me, and judge me not.' (p. 55)

'Oh, Elizabeth, your justice would freeze beer!' (p. 55)

'I see now your spirit twists around the single error of my life, and I will never tear it free.' (p. 61)

Although Elizabeth has, up to the moment she is arrested, been regarded in Salem as a woman of unimpeachable honesty, it is this

20th Century Fox/Everett/Rex Features

reputation that causes her husband to be condemned because she lies about his affair with Abigail, mistakenly thinking it will save him.

Elizabeth is presented at the start of Act Two as a cold and demanding woman, whose chilly demeanour may have driven her husband to adultery and whose continual suspicions of her husband render their marriage tense.

However, Miller develops Elizabeth's character beyond this. She is a shrewd judge of her husband. She recognises that much of his anger comes from his own harsh judgement of his poor behaviour with Abigail. Elizabeth tells him that it is not she that is judging him but that 'The magistrate sits in your heart that judges you' (p. 55). This idea is returned to at the end of the play when Elizabeth and John are briefly reunited before his execution. He again asks for her forgiveness and she tells him, 'John, it come to naught that I should forgive you, if you'll not forgive yourself' (p. 119).

In the end, we see that Elizabeth loves her husband deeply, but she held such a low opinion of herself that she never quite trusted him to love her as much as she did him. Almost her last words to him are 'Forgive me, forgive me, John — I never knew such goodness in the world!' (p. 119).

> **Key quotation**
>
> John, I counted myself so plain, so poorly made, no honest love could come to me! Suspicion kissed you when I did; I never knew how I should say my love. It were a cold house I kept!'
>
> (Elizabeth, p. 119)

> **Pause for thought**
>
> Read the moving scene between Proctor and Elizabeth in Act Four closely. With hindsight, what possible clues does Miller give us at this stage about what is driving Elizabeth's apparent 'coldness' towards her husband?

Reverend Samuel Parris

Miller describes Reverend Parris as 'a widower with no interest in children', 'and there is very little good to be said for him' (p. 13). He is a weak, bitter, fearful and suspicious man who, after first saying there can be no witchcraft in Salem, becomes active in keeping the trials going in order to safeguard his own name and position. He is both morally and practically weak: ready to condemn but not forgive others and constantly complaining about his finances and other material conditions. His fear and bitterness are both part of his nature and driven by the fact that his daughter is one of the girls who danced naked in the woods. He is continually beset with fears that others conspire against him.

It is almost certain that Parris knows that Abigail is lying about the dancing and the witchcraft, but he perpetuates the deception because it is in his own self-interest.

> **Pause for thought**
>
> Miller sets up Parris as a one-dimensional villain at the very start of the play. Do you think the story would be more effective if Parris had some decent and admirable qualities and his bad side were more slowly revealed? Why do you think Miller does not do this?

> **Key quotation**
>
> I want a mark of confidence, is all! I am your third preacher in seven years. I do not wish to be put out like the cat whenever some majority feels the whim.
>
> (Parris, p. 35)

He sees any challenges against charges of witchcraft as a personal attack on him as the spiritual leader of the community.

Miller gives Parris no qualities that we can absolutely say are those of a good man. The anxiety he shows for Betty at the start of the play is more likely to be worry that he will be tainted by accusations of witchcraft than a parent's concern for their child's health. At the end of the play, when he appears humbled and reduced, we might think this has been caused by a realisation of the injustices he has conspired in. Yet we quickly learn that he — already established as a man hugely concerned with worldly wealth — has had his savings stolen and is ruined. Miller wants us to see that it is financial loss rather than any guilt which has changed him.

Grade *booster*

Parris was a merchant in Barbados. Many people in the 1600s felt they had a lifelong 'calling' to serve God, but Parris was keen enough to make money as a merchant to go to Barbados before he became a reverend. Perhaps John Proctor is right when he says that Parris was constantly saying he wanted gold candlesticks for his church and that he, unlike the previous minister, insisted on rent-free accommodation.

Reverend John Hale

Reverend Hale comes to Salem on Reverend Parris's request to investigate possible supernatural causes for Betty Parris's suspicious illness. Parris invites Hale believing that he will clearly 'refute' any possible allegations of bewitching, but of course this quickly goes wrong and the witch hunt begins.

Hale arrives carrying heavy books and impresses people gathered at Parris's house with a speech about the power and truth these books contain. By our standards, and even by the standards of his own time in more liberal and enlightened communities, Hale's 'scholarship' is limited and crude.

Grade *booster*

Use the internet to research the advances in science and philosophy that were being made in Europe in the late 1600s. Find some key names, explore their ideas and compare their scholarship to Hale's witch-finding. Explain how Miller is using Hale's speeches in Act One about the power of his books to present Salem as a community that was not anywhere near the cutting edge of contemporary thought in the late 1600s.

Text **focus**

Hale is clearly enjoying being the centre of attention when he arrives with his books to help the residents of Salem seek out witchcraft. He tries to impress them with his learning with several speeches about witchcraft. He says, '*with a tasty love of intellectual pursuit*', ' Here is all the invisible world, caught, defined, and calculated. In these books the Devil stands stripped of all his brute disguises' (p. 42).

Hale's 'scholarship' supports the rumours of witchcraft and turns them into crimes to be sought out. Hale approaches the situation precisely and intellectually, believing that he can define the supernatural in definitive terms.

Hale is a major character both in what his actions cause to happen through the play and because Miller shows him as a man who undergoes a significant change as the play unfolds. Initially eager to seek out witches, by the end of Act Three he is driven to flee Salem because he is so horrified by what is happening. In Act Four he returns full of sympathy for the condemned and torn by doubt about the validity and truth of the witch hunt. He is tortured by his own guilt, by the powerful hand he's played in these many deaths.

> ### Key quotation
>
> **There is blood on my head! Can you not see the blood on my head!!**
> (Hale, p. 114)

> ### Pause for thought
>
> The nineteenth-century Irish politician Edmund Burke famously said, 'All that is required for evil to flourish in the world is for good men to do nothing.' How far do you think this might be true of Hale?

Abigail Williams

A 17-year-old girl who is the niece of Reverend Parris, Abigail was the Proctors' servant before Elizabeth threw her out for having an affair with John Proctor. Abigail is a malicious, vengeful and bullying girl who, in an attempt to protect herself from punishment after Reverend Parris finds her and others dancing in the woods, instigates the Salem witch trials and leads the flood of accusations.

Abigail is an unabashed liar who charges witchcraft against those who oppose her. She does this initially to save herself from punishment for dancing in the woods, but as the accusations begin to engulf the whole village, she appears to be acting out of a malicious delight in exerting power. She accuses Elizabeth Proctor in an attempt to make space for her to take Elizabeth's place as Proctor's wife, or at least his lover.

Miller adds depth and a hint of possible justification or even redemption to Abigail's character with the simple suggestion that her callous nature

> ### Pause for thought
>
> Abigail is described as a beauty. What elements of her role in the play would be brought alive by the appearance of an appropriately attractive actor playing Abigail on stage? (This is a good example of how a play and its characters only reach full potential when acted on stage.)

stems partially from past trauma; she is an orphan who watched as her parents were murdered by Indians.

Abigail will become the ringleader of the girls. We see her powerful nature in Act One. She becomes angry when questioned by her uncle, and later plays the ringleader to make her position secure. These moments early in the play set up her desire to control situations.

In-depth analysis of Abigail and the other girls should include the idea that all this has come about through the repression of individual expression in Salem. The girls express their youthfulness through dancing in the woods because they cannot express themselves publicly in a sombre world where dancing is seen as sinful.

Pause for thought

What is the symbolic importance of the forest being the place where the dancing takes place?

Supporting characters

Thomas Putnam

One of the wealthiest landowners in Salem, Thomas Putnam is a vindictive, bitter man who holds long-standing grudges against many of the citizens of Salem, including the Nurse family for blocking the appointment of his brother-in-law to the position of minister. Putnam pushes his daughter (whom we don't actually see) to charge witchcraft against George Jacobs, for if he is executed, his land will be available for Putnam to purchase. He will buy the land cheaply as it will be auctioned, and we're informed that only Putnam has the money to buy, so there won't be anyone else bidding against him. (Corey outwits him in the end by refusing to say 'aye' or 'nay' to the charges against him — so that his land has to go to his sons by law.)

Ann Putnam

The wife of Thomas Putnam, Ann suspects that there is some paranormal reason for the deaths of her seven children, who all died 'before they live a day'. She hints that she blames Rebecca Nurse. She is a bitter and angry woman. Miller gives us no glimpse of any more humane, redemptive qualities, even though the death of so many babies — due to some tragic medical error or condition in her — could otherwise allow us to have some sympathy for Ann Putnam.

Rebecca Nurse

One of the most noble, kind, reasonable and well-respected citizens of Salem, this elderly woman suggests that Betty's illness is simply a natural part of growing up. She is a sensible woman and understands how manipulative children can be without realising the extent of damage that their mischief can cause.

However, because she served as midwife to Mrs Putnam, she is charged with the supernatural murder of Putnam's children. Rebecca Nurse is the nearest character to a martyr in the play, the most pure and saintly character hanged for witchcraft. Her bravery in the face of death is an inspiration to John Proctor, causing him to face his own death rather than betray innocent people with a false confession and accusations.

Mary Warren

The 18-year-old servant in the Proctor household, Mary is one of the girls caught dancing in the woods with Abigail. She is complicit in Abigail Williams' schemes. Although weak and tentative, she challenges the Proctors in Act Two when they forbid her to go to court. However, Mary eventually breaks down and testifies against Abigail until Abigail pretends that Mary is using witchcraft against her (pp. 101–02).

> **Key quotation**
>
> **Oh, Mary, this is a black art to change your shape. No, I cannot, I cannot stop my mouth; it's God's work I do.**
>
> (Abigail, p. 101)

Mary Warren faces Judge Danforth. Describe the emotions that the faces of the other girls convey in this scene.

20th Century Fox/Everett/Rex Features

At this point Mary loses her nerve and once more follows Abigail's lead, as she can see that if she doesn't, she too will be condemned. Mary is a pliable girl whose actions are easily steered by others.

Giles Corey

An irascible and combative elderly resident of Salem, Giles Corey is the nearest thing to a comic figure in *The Crucible*. However, his fate turns to tragedy when he unwittingly brings down a charge of witchcraft on his own wife. In the presence of Hale arriving with his books, Corey wonders aloud about the strange books his wife reads at night. He thinks he finds it hard to pray after his wife has been reading.

Corey is a frequent plaintiff in court, having brought dozens of lawsuits, and he stands with Proctor in challenging the girls' accusations, believing that Thomas Putnam is using charges of witchcraft to secure land.

When Corey refuses to name the person who, he says, heard Putnam declare these intentions, Corey is charged with contempt of court and dies because, as Elizabeth tells her husband in Act Four, 'He would not answer aye or nay to his indictment; for if he denied the charge they'd hang him surely, and auction out his property' (pp. 117–18). Miller tells us that Giles has been in court many times and developed some knowledge of the law. He uses this to outwit those who want his land, though he pays with his life.

Deputy Governor Danforth

The deputy governor of the province of Massachusetts, Danforth presides over the Salem witch trials. He is the most senior authority figure in the play. He is a stern yet practical man, finally revealed as being more interested in preserving firstly his own dignity and then that of the court than in executing justice or behaving with any sense of fairness.

He approaches the witchcraft trials with a strict adherence to rules and law that obscures any sense of rationality, for under his legal dictates an accusation of witchcraft automatically entails a conviction unless the accused confesses then claims conversion back to God.

However by Act Four, Danforth shows that his greatest interest – overriding justice – is preserving, first, his own reputation, then the authority of the court. He has come to see himself as the human embodiment of the court, so that an attack on its processes and judgement is taken as a personal attack.

Danforth prompts Proctor to sign a confession, then to name others whom Proctor will have to say falsely are in league with the Devil. Here in Act Four, Danforth is a perfect example of the kind of man who, throughout history, has committed injustices claiming that they were acting according to their religious or political duty. The history of the Christian church is full of massacres and atrocities committed against non-believers 'in God's name'; while the enforcers and torturers of repressive political regimes have often said, when brought to trial, that they believed they were doing their duty to the state.

> **Key quotation**
>
> **Postponement now speaks a floundering on my part...**
> (Danforth, p. 113)

> **Key quotation**
>
> **Now draw yourselves up like men and help me, as you are bound by Heaven to do.**
> (Danforth, p. 113)

Text focus

When Danforth first appears (p. 78), Miller presents him as a man of intelligence and reason who might just have sufficient open-mindedness to call a halt to the trials. Miller describes him as 'a grave man in his sixties, of some humour and sophistication', but then he balances this by saying that this quality 'does not, however, interfere with an exact loyalty to his position and his cause'. 'Loyalty to his position' is a fascinating phrase that is full of information for us and for the actor playing Danforth. It suggests a man in thrall to his own authority, which in many less serious plays is a key trait of a foolish person full of self-importance and lacking perception. This description subtly creates a character who will become the most chilling of all the prosecutors, insisting on executions in Act Four even though everyone, including himself, is beginning to believe that the girls have lied.

> **Pause for thought**
>
> Find places in Acts Three and Four where Danforth appears ready to 'see sense' and declare the whole witch hunt a fake. What happens? Why do you think Miller gives Danforth these moments?

Judge Hathorne

Hathorne is the judge who presides over the Salem witch trials with Deputy Governor Danforth. He remains largely subservient to Danforth, but applies the same blinkered, prejudiced reasoning to charges of witchcraft. He appears to lack his superior's intelligence and potential capacity for more humane analysis.

Ezekiel Cheever

Cheever is a clerk of the court who serves the arrest warrants to the persons charged with witchcraft. He is an example of an ordinary person who gains status during the witch hunts, and who, like Danforth, assists in undertaking injustices believing it is his duty. Danforth may be guilty of the greater crime of sitting in judgement over the innocent, but without the actions of minor officials like Cheever the trials would not operate.

Minor characters

Betty Parris

The ten-year-old daughter of Reverend Parris, Betty falls mysteriously ill after Reverend Parris catches her dancing in the woods with Abigail and some girls and other young women of Salem. She only appears in Act One, where she has a few lines. She goes into real or feigned hysterics when she hears the name of Jesus sung by people downstairs below her bedroom.

> **Pause for thought**
>
> In the prose interlude on the first page of the text, Miller describes Betty's father as a man with 'no interest in children, or talent with them'. Later we learn that some people in Salem fear to take their children to hear Parris preach because he talks so much about Hell. What kind of parent do you think Parris has been? How might this influence Betty's behaviour now?

We suspect that Betty is terrified of Abigail, who is in the bedroom, but it could be that she is suffering from some fever which Abigail exploits as a way of avoiding confessing the 'sin' of leading the girls to dance naked in the woods.

Tituba

Parris's slave from Barbados, Tituba was with the girls when they danced and attempted to conjure the spirits of Ann Putnam's dead children. She is the first person accused of witchcraft and the first person to accuse others — particularly when she discovers that the easiest way to spare herself is to admit to the charges, no matter their truth. She is clearly the outsider in this community. She is not developed to any great extent by Miller; her function in the play is to remind us how frightened, bigoted, over-organised communities ignore or abuse others who are 'not like them' with no sense of conscience or guilt. On the allegorical level at which the play operates, Miller wants us to see in Tituba an example of the kind of person whom the House Committee on Un-American Activities was harassing in 1950s America. People born outside the USA were particularly suspected by the committee.

Text focus

Tituba's speech on p. 48 is the only one in the play not written in the biblically inspired language that Miller creates for all the puritans. It has a warmth and life lacking in everyone else's speeches. It is also mocking — intentionally or not — of the chilly and unfriendly solemnity that the puritans surround themselves with.

Tituba's speech also gives a 'reason' for why she might work for the Devil, which is bigger and bolder than the petty accusations and confessions of the puritans. Tituba claims the Devil offered to set her free, to buy her a pretty dress — something she would never have as a slave in a rigorous puritan community — and take her home. It is a convincing set of reasons to impress the people who have enslaved her. She says that the Devil told her: 'You work for me, Tituba, and I make you free! I give you pretty dress to wear, and put you way high up in the air, and you gone fly back to Barbados.'

Mercy Lewis

Mercy Lewis is the Putnams' servant — a fat, sly, merciless 18-year-old girl whom Parris found naked when he caught the girls dancing in the woods. She runs away with Abigail at the end of the play.

Francis Nurse

The husband of Rebecca Nurse, and a well-respected wealthy landowner in Salem, Francis Nurse joins Giles Corey and John Proctor to challenge the court when their wives are charged with witchcraft.

Marshall Herrick

Marshal Herrick is one of the local constables. He is drunk on duty while he guards the women in jail. He offers them drink. He is a disreputable character who gives a further unsavoury air to the trials. There was more than a hint of sexual perversion in the whole world-wide issue of men seeing women as witches: imprisoning, torturing, burning and hanging them. Miller is not making any clear link between men seeking judicial and spiritual power over women and a desire for sexual dominance in this play, but at the start of this act it is present as a dark undercurrent. The fact that Marshal Herrick, the jailor, is drunk and lets the women drink from his bottle adds to the tension of the scene and our unease.

Sarah Good

One of the first women charged with witchery by the girls, Sarah is a homeless woman who confesses to witchcraft to save herself and continues the charade with Tituba at the start of Act Four, comically claiming that Satan will take her and Tituba to Barbados.

Susanna Walcott

Susanna is one of the girls whom Parris found dancing in the woods, and a confidante of Abigail.

Hopkins

Hopkins is a guard at the Salem jail.

Review your learning

(Answers on p. 88)

1. Explain how the affair that John Proctor has had with Abigail before the play begins is crucial to the plot.

2. Describe the relationship between John and Elizabeth Proctor. How does it develop and change through the play?

3. Miller is keen to show that some characters have contrasting key elements to their personalities. Explain these two different sides to Giles Corey and to Hale.

4. What is it that is known about the character of Elizabeth Proctor that makes the judges place her so she cannot be seen by her husband, nor he see her, when they question her in Act Three?

More interactive questions and answers online.

Themes

- **What is a theme?**
- **What are the key themes of *The Crucible*?**
- **How do the themes link to one another?**
- **How are the themes explored through the actions and motives of the characters?**

Themes are the universal and fundamental ideas explored in a literary work. They underlie the story. In studying *The Crucible*, you might call them the messages that Miller wants the audience to think about, over and above the events in the historical story being told.

There are several key, linked themes underlying the events of *The Crucible*. Miller explores these themes through the motives of the characters and the actions they take or are affected by. All good drama engages us with its themes by drawing us into a story that includes characters we care about or are angered by, and so on. Unlike a novel, where the author can explain directly to their readers what ideas are being explored, in a play we have only the words and actions of the characters to lead us into thinking about themes behind the story.

Authority and dissent

There are many levels of authority within the world of the play. At the start of Act One, Reverend Parris is the sole voice of spiritual authority in Salem. He is the appointed minister and a graduate of Harvard College. However, his fear of his family being tainted with claims of witchcraft and his natural lack of leadership qualities mean that he is quickly supplanted by the arrival of Reverend Hale. Hale is proud to show how he derives his authority from books and learning. He stresses this much more than any personal claims to spirituality or righteousness.

By the end of Act Three, Hale is shown to be a man capable of recognising doubt and trying to halt unjust courses of action, but his authority is in turn supplanted by the judges, their court and its officials. Although they are leaders in their community, Danforth and Hathorne lack the local knowledge of Parris and the 'specialised knowledge' of investigating witchcraft possessed by Hale.

The judges' primary role in the play is to be strict enforcers of law. Danforth may like to be seen as having a sharp legal mind, but his one

> **Pause for thought**
>
> What effect does this constant 'scaling up' of authority figures have on the witch trials? How do you think it affects the girls?

> **Key quotation**
>
> But witchcraft is *ipso facto*, on its face and by its nature, an invisible crime, is it not? Therefore, who may possibly be witness to it?
>
> (Danforth, p. 90)

demonstrated argument against Mary Corey's claim to know that she isn't a witch at the start of Act Three is logically simplistic.

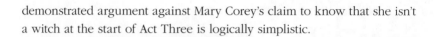
The rest of the time, Danforth and Hathorne merely impose law or ask simple questions, often loaded with threats, to gain the answers they want to hear. As the ultimate and final figures of authority, Danforth and Hathorne are strict, unbending and unable or unwilling to entertain doubts. Coupled with their unwavering strict religious views, these qualities make them emblematic of the kind of people who have committed atrocities and injustices in the name of different beliefs throughout history. Miller wants us constantly to see the judges as historical parallels to the figures who were conducting 'witch hunts' of a different sort against suspected communists on behalf of the House Committee on Un-American Activities.

Danforth is at his most chilling at the end of the play, where he is prepared to continue with trials and executions even though the community is being destroyed by endless accusations and some people fear a rebellion. He demands that John Proctor denounce others as part of his confession. He will not accept the confession without further names of innocent people. Miller wanted to show Danforth as the worst sort of authority figure: a man who justifies his perpetrating violence and injustice by claiming that it is the will of God and so his duty.

Against these authority figures are set two characters who lead dissent. Proctor and Giles Corey are individualists who rebel under these layers of authority. Proctor has rejected Parris's preaching and his spiritual authority, and rarely attends church. Corey made the authority of the law work for him as a constant plaintiff in court cases resulting from disputes between himself and his neighbours. The individualistic behaviour of these men might have been tolerated in the past, but the 'emergency' of the witch trials — combined with a sense that the community is rotten with too strict and invasive moral principles — creates a situation where such dissent against official authority is going to lead Proctor and Corey into trouble. Both men are killed by state-sanctioned, unjust murders. They are the two most modern figures in the play for their willingness to push back against the extreme authority of the courts. Miller wants us to connect with them and their ways of thinking more than any other characters in the play.

Intolerance

The Crucible is set in a theocratic society: that is, a community in which the church and the state are one. Laws are created that are based on religious principles and these govern how people should act. In most present-day western countries, and many others all over the world based on democratic principles, religion has very little influence on the laws that people live by. There may sometimes be some influence: the laws of the Republic of Ireland, a largely Catholic country, banned abortions — which Catholic teaching forbids — until constitutional referendums in 1992 and 2002 used public opinion to drive new laws allowing abortions in some situations. As late as 1957, the Irish courts hanged a woman who helped another try to abort a child and the pregnant woman died. In many Islamic countries, the rules of religion do shape the laws by which everyone lives. This kind of Islamic law is called sharia.

Salem's community is built upon everyone following a strict, austere form of Protestantism known as Puritanism. Puritans believed in a strong moral code that governed all behaviour in public and private life. Many historians believe it was this total conformity and sense of 'being right' that allowed puritan colonies in America in the late 1600s to survive in the face of dangers and adversities when other more liberal and individualist early settlements failed.

Salem had been established for just 40 years at the time the play is set. Some people were beginning to question if such strict rules were still needed. People wanted more individual freedom, but were terrified of being denounced by others as challenging both the law and God's word, which they believed underpinned the law.

In a theocratic society like Salem, private sins and the status of every individual's soul could become matters of public concern. This sense of being under constant scrutiny is increased by the smallness of the community and its isolation. There is no room for deviation from social norms, since any individual whose private life doesn't conform to the established moral laws represents a threat to public order and the rule of God and true religion. In Salem, everything and everyone belongs to either God or the Devil.

> **Pause for thought**
>
> Describe clearly in no more than two or three sentences why you think communities like Salem would survive in the face of adversity. How would they act?

> **Key quotation**
>
> **Let you counsel among yourselves; think on your village and what may have drawn from heaven such thundering wrath upon you all.**
>
> (Hale, p. 73)

Dissent is associated with Satanic activity. There can be no tolerance of different views. This drives the underlying logic behind the witch trials, which is summed up by Danforth's pronouncement: '…a person is either with this court or he must be counted against it'.

The witch trials are the ultimate expression of intolerance. Executing witches is the ultimate means of restoring the community's purity. The trials brand all social deviants with the taint of Devil-worship and demand their elimination. This process continues even when so many people have been 'eliminated' that the economy and life of Salem is under threat. Finally, after 19 hangings and Giles Corey's 'pressing' to death, the community begins to rebel. The end of the witch trials (which happens shortly after the play closes with John Proctor's death) marked a change in the way Salem was governed, and greater personal freedoms began to develop.

Hysteria

Miller wanted to show how group hysteria, if allowed to go unchecked by reason, can tear a community apart. He wanted audiences to make an instant connection with what he regarded as the mass hysteria gripping 1950s America in its search for suspected communist sympathisers.

The girls out in the woods. What do you think made the girls want to go and dance in the woods and pretend to raise spirits?

We might think the girls' group delusions or scheming to be obviously false and ridiculous, but the Salem puritans believed in the capacity of women to become witches and do the Devil's work, up to and including murder by spells and curses.

20th Century Fox/Everett/Rex Features

As the denouncements increase, hysteria supplants logic and enables people to believe that neighbours, most of whom they have always considered upstanding people, are committing absurd and unbelievable crimes.

Grade *booster*

A high-scoring essay on *The Crucible* would explain how Miller needs to create a climax at the end of each act, so that we look forward with anticipation to what will happen next. In the space of just over a page at the end of Act One, the Devil is mentioned 11 times. Everyone's lines are short and simple statements. The effect is to create hurry, panic and excitement.

Miller adds human greed to this picture of a community beset by constant squabbles and unresolved feuds, so that being able to denounce a minor enemy becomes an attractive possibility for unscrupulous and bitter people who want to gain land and power.

There are many examples of this behaviour through the play. The Putnams have their daughter denounce the Coreys with the aim of buying their land if they are condemned and their property is taken in forfeit by the court. Abigail is both the main engineer of the hysteria and someone who uses this to attempt to gain her own private ends. She accuses Elizabeth Proctor of witchcraft, believing that if Elizabeth is out of the way, either in jail or preferably dead, John Proctor will become her lover again. Parris attempts to strengthen his position in Salem by making scapegoats of people like Proctor who question his authority.

Miller exposes the unjust motives of all these people. He wants us to see that, in the end, hysteria in public life thrives only because unscrupulous people benefit from it.

> **Key quotation**
>
> **If Jacobs hangs for a witch he forfeit up his property — that's law! And there is none but Putnam with the coin to buy so great a piece.**
>
> (Giles, p. 87)

Reputation

Maintaining a reputation as a moral and religious person is tremendously important to people in theocratic Salem. Public and private moralities are one entity, and the situation has become so intense by the time the play begins that almost anyone feels able to investigate and criticise anyone else's private behaviour.

This sense of being able to pry into private lives drives Hale's unannounced visit to the Proctors' farmhouse in Act Two, which quickly becomes an interrogation of husband and wife in their own home. Although John Proctor becomes angry when his wife is arrested, for some time he allows Hale to question him and his wife. He may feel this is the safest course

> **Pause for thought**
>
> What effect is created by setting Act One in a bedroom, then filling it with people from outside the family? How do many of these people behave?

of action; he may also recognise that in Salem's ultra-religious society a reverend has the right to do this to him.

In a community where reputation plays such an important role, fear of guilt by association becomes very powerful. People are so desperate to maintain a righteous public image that they fear the sins of their friends and associates will taint their names.

Many characters are motivated by a desire to protect their reputations. At the start of the play, Parris fears that Abigail's increasingly questionable actions, and the hints of witchcraft surrounding his daughter's coma, will threaten his reputation as the town's spiritual leader. Meanwhile, the play's main protagonist, John Proctor, although one of the most individualistic of the characters in the play, seeks to keep his good name from being tarnished. In Act Two he has a chance to put a stop to the girls' accusations, but his desire to preserve his reputation keeps him from testifying against Abigail.

At the end of the play, however, Proctor's desire to keep his good name leads him to make the heroic choice not to make a false confession or to name other innocent people as being under the spell of witchcraft. He goes to his death rather than sign his name to an untrue statement. He says, 'I have given you my soul; leave me my name!' (p. 124). Proctor is now keener to have his reputation kept intact in the eyes of God than in the eyes of the judges in Salem.

Gaining empowerment

In many societies in different periods of history, people lacking social status, power or authority have used extreme circumstances and 'emergencies' that suspend usual laws and rules as opportunities to gain power. Empowerment is different from the personal gain that motivates other characters: empowerment is about gaining standing and authority in a usually strict and repressive community.

The witch trials empower several characters in *The Crucible*. In all cases, however, this empowerment is temporary.

Women and especially girls occupy the lowest social rung of highly conformist, male-dominated Salem. They have few options in life. They work as servants for families until they are old enough to be married off and have children of their own. Then, like all wives, they will be known as 'goody', short for 'good wife'. There is no other type of life available to women who want to remain part of the community: certainly no sort of career or role in the administration of the community. The only women in the play who are not living the conventional life of a 'good wife' are the slave Tituba and the wandering, aged beggar Goody Osburn.

Abigail has also fallen out of the conventional role that a young woman is supposed to have in Salem. Since being sacked by the Proctors, she cannot find work as a servant with any other family. She rebels against the code of this repressive society by seeking to express her sexuality and leading the others in their naked dancing in the woods. Abigail is the essence of everything that single women would be demonised for by the Salem community.

Grade *booster*

You will gain a higher mark in an examination if you can show how Miller builds into some of his characters elements that prevent them from being too one-dimensional. Abigail Williams could be described as a vain, spiteful and manipulative young girl who causes nothing but trouble. But Miller also makes her a victim of John Proctor's sexual whims. In the end, however, Abigail shows her true nature by running away from the horrors she has caused, stealing her uncle's cashbox and ruining him.

For Salem puritans, those who give themselves to the Devil are the ultimate example of people turning their back on God, so Abigail's accusations of witchcraft and Devil-worship immediately command the attention of the court. By aligning herself, in the eyes of others, with God's will, she gains a temporary power over adult society, as do the other girls. Their accusations quickly become virtually unassailable. Tituba, whose status is lower than that of anyone else in the play because she is a black slave, deflects blame from herself by accusing others, but she ends up condemned to hang.

Sin and guilt

Miller shows that the witch hunt was an opportunity for the repressed members of Salem society to publicly proclaim both their own sins and the sins of others. Guilt has been bottled up like terrible private secrets in this community, and the airing of sins and grievances is a relief to those previously without an outlet for confession. Guilt motivates not only the witch hunts themselves, but also the behaviour of several principal characters. Proctor is haunted by guilt over his infidelity, while, later in the play, Reverend Hale works to undermine the court that he helped create as penance for his sins. By the end of the play, the guilt he feels for the sins he has committed in pursuing the witch hunts has utterly changed and humbled him.

Miller, forever drawing a parallel between the witch hunts and the hunt for suspected communists in 1950s America, is keen to ensure that the play delivers the final irony of the Salem witch hunts: that the wrongs and injustices committed, the sins of the trials, quickly outpaced the alleged crimes, because there was no actual crime to begin with. The final, most important fact to take away from the Salem witch trials is that everyone who died was innocent.

Self-interest

All the instigators of the witch trials are working to serve their own self-interest to varying degrees. Abigail begins the hysteria when she finds it a convenient way to deflect attention from her own 'crimes'. Seeing how successful this is, she then accuses Elizabeth as a way of advancing her dream of being with John Proctor as his lover or even future wife. Tituba, the first person to be accused, is also the first to confess when she realises (incorrectly, as it turns out in her case) that confession will save her life. Parris at first argues against witchcraft being present, because it would undermine his reputation in the town. Even Giles Corey dies in the way he does because it is in his own interest — by not pleading and dying under the weighted rocks, he ensures that his property will pass to his sons rather than to the state.

Self-interest and self-defence motivate people accused by the courts to name others. This makes them appear to be cooperating with the court. By requiring the accused to name others in their confessions, a witch hunt (or indeed the investigative work of the House Committee on Un-American Activities) can take on the form of a pyramid scheme or chain letter. To avoid punishment, you must pass it on. This 'naming of names' allows accusations to spread through a community, while also permitting the public airing of grievances and sins.

As someone who found himself on the House Committee on Un-American Activities blacklist, Miller felt particularly strongly about the evil of accusing others to save oneself, and he expresses this idea by having several characters in the play grapple with the requirement that they name names. Giles Corey is held in contempt — the charge that ultimately leads to his execution — for refusing to name the person who told him of Putnam's scheming. Proctor baulks at the court's intention to question the 91 people who signed a declaration of his good character. Finally, Proctor would rather die than accuse more innocent people.

Pause for thought

Make a list of characters (it will be very short) who appear to act without any self-interest at all.

Review your learning

(Answers on p. 88)

1. Make a list of figures in the play who, from the start, are symbols of authority. Beside each, write a line explaining the kind of authority they have.
   Now list the main characters who stand up to and challenge authority. Rank them according to how much you think they stand up to the rule of authority.

2. Why does Miller need to show us two instances of the girls' hysterical 'performances'? Where do these occur and what specific dramatic purpose do they each fulfil in the unfolding story?

3. List the characters who gain any form of empowerment as events unfold in Salem, and explain what each gains.

4. Which characters in the play are motivated purely by self-interest? Beside each name, explain very briefly what it is they hope to gain by events.

More interactive questions and answers online.

Style

- What is the overall style of the language of the play?
- What meanings should we look for in the dialogue between characters?
- How does Miller create a voice for each main character?
- How are motives and emotions revealed through what characters say?

Miller's choice of a way of speaking for the characters

Playwrights don't speak directly to their audience: everything they want to say has to come through the mouths of their characters. The added complication with this play is that Miller has created a highly stylised language for all the characters. This is based on the language of the King James Bible, which was the version that the Salem puritans would hear read aloud and quoted.

We don't actually know how people in Salem in 1692 spoke to one another, but when we hear the actors speaking their lines, we know they sound very different from us. They load their speech with biblical and religious images and ideas, and this works as far as it needs to for dramatic effect in a very stylised and emotionally charged and intense play.

Religious references and constant mentions of duty and of being the right sort of God-fearing person are spoken by all characters in almost all situations. This is because there is little cultural input in their lives apart from the Bible. They do not appear to speak very differently when in private or in public. Again Miller is showing how the constant demand to conform to religious principles creates people who appear — or actually are — one-dimensional. Characters in *The Crucible* face real and terrifying moral dilemmas and choices, but their language always remains filled with the rhetoric of Christianity. The effect is to suggest that they are people unhealthily obsessed with one set of principles.

Reading a play

Playwrights cannot develop an authorial voice like novelists, who can speak directly to their readers. They cannot write lengthy descriptions of events and scenes, analyse motives or give us an 'overview' of characters' inner lives.

This play is very unusual, however, because Miller provides people reading the text (as opposed to seeing a production) with a number of prose passages within the script, in which he lays out his reasons for writing the play, provides additional background information on Salem and the puritan community, and introduces several of the main characters. (See the end of this section for more details on these prose passages.)

Plays usually consist almost entirely of lines for a cast of actors to speak. The only non-spoken parts in the text of a play are descriptions of the set, stage directions to tell actors about any special moves and their entrances and exits, and line directions, usually only included if a line has to be said in a particular way that is not obvious from the content and context of the line.

Pause for thought

Look through the play and note some of the line directions that Miller gives. How do they help you 'hear' the play in your head? What examples can you give where a direction adds real meaning to your understanding of a line and of the situation in which it is said?

The people of Salem are mainly farmers. Any education they have had will be focused on reading and learning the Bible and other Christian texts. None of them, not even Hale or Danforth, is an intellectual in any sense that we would understand. Their language is therefore basic. No one engages in long philosophical arguments, tells a lengthy story, describes any event or scene in a lyrical or poetic way, or references any material beyond their lives except Christian beliefs. The main characteristic of their language is that it appears over-emotional and 'overheated'. While it is true that all drama is based on conflict, and of course all good dramatic writing has to be full of drama (imagine a play where people just sat and chatted in a friendly way!), nonetheless almost every exchange in this play quickly descends into argument, accusation or confession.

The main 'decorations' to this basic and plain language are Christian references and excessive symbolism. Much of this also seems rather frantic and overheated. Ann Putnam is horrified by whatever it is she feels is happening in the village and describes these nameless (and of course unfounded) fears by saying 'There are wheels within wheels in this village, and fires within fires!' (p. 33). Hale uses a great deal of symbolism in the play, all of it referring to the Bible or other Christian texts. His warning to Elizabeth Proctor, 'cleave to no faith when faith brings blood' (p. 115), could sum up the warning of the whole play: that belief can breed fanaticism and fanaticism breeds the capacity for cruelty.

The narrative interludes

Miller provides people reading the text of the play with the following prose sections:

- an overture laying out the world of the play (pp. 13–17)
- a prose introduction and analysis of Thomas Putnam (pp. 22–23)
- a prose introduction of John Proctor (p. 27)
- 'a word' for Rebecca (Nurse) (pp. 31–32)
- a prose introduction and analysis of Hale, and further background to the themes of the play (pp. 36–40)
- a prose introduction and analysis of Giles Corey (pp. 43–44)
- 'Echoes down the corridor' — a short prose passage briefly describing what happened after the moment at which the play ends (p. 127)

Careful reading of these prose interludes will help you understand why Miller wrote the play and why he created some of the key characters.

In these prose interludes, Miller establishes the particular quality of Salem society that makes it especially susceptible to the repression and panic of the witch trials. He explores some of the key characters, to provide us with further understanding of the community in which the play unfolds. He explains the particular circumstances and historical events upon which it is closely based.

Miller created the prose interludes because he was very keen that everyone understood his reasons for choosing to write about a distant and uniquely horrible set of events in American history. He wanted to ensure that they understood the exact natures and motives of all the key characters he was creating. However, the interludes do, of course, interrupt the flow of the narrative and break our concentration on the world of Salem and the unfolding story.

All the prose passages are cut from stage productions, though some directors use all or some of them as notes in the programme available for audience members to buy.

Review your learning

(Answers on p. 89)

1 Why do so many of the characters have a similar way of speaking?

2 Find examples of imagery which characters use to bring out the 'fire, wrath and damnation' aspect of their religion and anger in their personal feelings. Now look for similar imagery used to express love, joy and tenderness. What are you finding as you build this second list?

3 There is little description of everyday transactions, events and scenes anywhere in the play. Each act is full of anger and bitterness. Identify any key features of language that Miller uses to convey this anger and bitterness.

More interactive questions and answers online.

Assessment Objectives and skills

- What are the Assessment Objectives?
- What do they mean?
- How does the assessor decide how well you have met them?
- What skills can you develop to help you prove to the assessor that you are targeting these areas well?

What are the Assessment Objectives?

Assessment Objectives, or AOs as they are called, are the particular criteria that you must target in your written responses. The number of marks you are awarded will relate directly to how well you have met these 'objectives' or criteria. These AOs are identical, no matter which board you are being assessed by.

Do the AOs vary between foundation and higher tiers?

This question only applies to AQA, as for Edexcel the unit covering *The Crucible* is tierless. For AQA students, then, the simple answer is no; the assessment objectives are identical for both tiers. The foundation tier is made 'easier' by the phrasing of the questions and the fact that bullet-pointed hints will help to form a framework that you can use in constructing your answer. (See the next chapter for examples of foundation- and higher-tier-style questions.)

The AOs as presented by the examination boards

AO1

Respond to texts critically and imaginatively; select and evaluate relevant textual detail to illustrate and support interpretations.

AO2

Explain how language, structure and form contribute to writers' presentation of ideas, themes and settings.

AO3

Make comparisons and explain links between texts, evaluating writers' different ways of expressing meaning and achieving effects.

AO4

Relate texts to their social, cultural and historical contexts; explain how texts have been influential and significant to self and other readers in different contexts and at different times.

What the AOs mean and how to meet them

First, a health warning: these AOs are presented separately by the examination boards, but when you are writing your responses, you will not be able to (and nor should you try to) separate them entirely. All that you need to concentrate upon is answering the question, or addressing the task squarely and fully, as these are designed by the examination boards to ensure that, provided you do this, you cannot avoid hitting the AOs that they are focusing upon in this unit.

AO1

What your assessors are looking for here is how far you have reached an understanding of why Miller might have written this play. What point, or points, do you think he might have been trying to convey and why? You will convince your assessor that you have reached some thoughtful and valid conclusions by supporting your arguments with close references to Miller's play. The part of your analysis that will gain you the highest marks will be the quality of the explanation that you offer about the references you make; why they have made you think as you do about what Miller might have been wishing to say.

This is the only AO you are assessed on by Edexcel when writing about this play (see p. 71 for more about this).

The following two examples of meeting AO1 focus on the idea of personal vengeance in *The Crucible.*

Meeting AO1: example 1

Miller clearly wishes to expose the way the witch hunts in Salem, just like the McCarthy 'witch-hunts' for communists in his own time, resulted in 'long-held hatreds of neighbours…being openly expressed, and vengeance taken', in the shape of accusations that the accused had no way of proving false. Also in his overture, Miller states that 'suspicions and the envy of the miserable toward the happy could and did burst out in the general revenge'. It is no accident that Miller

Grade *booster*

Stay entirely focused on key elements of your task or question throughout your response and you will hit the necessary AOs. The level of your mark will depend on the depth of your analysis.

Grade *booster*

Notice how PEE is being used in these examples (see next chapter to for a fuller illustration of how to use this technique).

has chosen Salem in 1692 as the setting for his play; what he is saying is that McCarthyism was as ill-founded and explosively dangerous as the witch-hunts of this earlier era were in providing individuals with an official excuse to avenge themselves upon their neighbours by pointing the finger of accusation at them.

Here the student makes references to the play to support their view that the play mirrors events in Miller's own society, with similar outcomes. This is also a good example of how knowing the context (AO4) can inform your understanding of the play. This example also shows an understanding of an aspect of AO2, as the student is talking about the effects on the audience of Miller's choice of **setting**.

Grade *booster*

Notice too in these examples that the quotation is short, and smoothly embedded so that it reads as an integral part of the student's sentence.

Meeting AO1: example 2

Miller uses the character of Giles Corey to help him to illustrate how this sort of political climate lays individuals wide open to abuses such as that voiced by Giles in Act Three when he tells Danforth of a man accused of witchcraft by Putnam, reminding him that if he is convicted, his land will be 'forfeit' and that there is 'none but Putnam with the coin' to purchase it. Miller makes starkly clear how lethal this avenue to abuse of one's neighbours was, when he has Corey exclaim, 'This man is killing his neighbours for their land!'

AO2

- **Form** refers to overall shape. In this case it refers to the genre the writer has used; here, a play. Understanding of form might include an awareness of how characters are created and used in order to convey the playwright's themes; how settings are created; how sound effects or lighting are used, and the use of colour. Notice how, with a play, much is to do with playing upon the senses of the audience; what they see, hear and feel through the atmosphere created in the theatre.
- **Language** refers to what the characters are given by the writer to say, and how they say it.
- **Structure** refers to the way in which the play is put together: for example, the order in which events occur or in which characters are introduced, or when and how characters make their exits and entrances.

Grade *booster*

Show your assessor that you understand that the play is a construct of the writer, through which he is conveying his thoughts and ideas to his audience, by remembering to foreground his name often, as is done in the examples.

You will need to refer to examples of the above in Miller's play to show that you understand how his use of these dramatic techniques has shaped your understanding of the play.

Remember that AQA will be assessing you on AO2 as well as AO1 (see the next chapter for more information about this.)

The following two examples of meeting AO2 focus on Miller's building of tension.

Meeting AO2: example 1

When Miller first introduces Abigail, it is with the direction that she is 'strikingly beautiful…with an endless capacity for dissembling'. It is important that the actress playing Abigail be able to put this across in the early scenes between her, Betty Parris and John Proctor, so that the audience understands fully the danger she represents for Mary Warren and Proctor in Act Three. When Abigail is exposed by Mary Warren and Proctor as a 'whore' who 'thinks to dance with me on my wife's grave', the audience's prior knowledge of her powers of manipulation increases the tension in the auditorium; her warning to Danforth, 'Let you beware, Mr Danforth', further raises this tension and it reaches a peak when Abigail begins to fake her possession by spirits again. Miller stresses her total believ-ability when he directs, 'Suddenly, from an accusatory attitude, her face turns, looking into the air above — it is truly frightened.' From this alone, the audience will be aware that Mary Warren will not be able to hold out against her accusa-tions and at this point the frustration in the audience at the gullibility of these court officials would be reaching an almost unbearable point.

Here the student has made clear their understanding of how the way in which a character is delineated (revealed to the audience at different points within the play) is important in feeding into and illustrating the themes of the playwright.

Meeting AO2: example 2

This tension reaches a climax when Abigail cries out, 'Oh, Heavenly Father, take away this shadow!', and Miller has Proctor 'leap' at Abigail, 'without warning or hesitation', grab her by her hair and pull her to her feet. These violent and dramatic actions along with his accusation of her being a 'whore' whip the tension up to a climax, when Miller begins to release it by having Proctor finally say, 'I have made a bell of my honour! I have rung the doom of my good name.' His choice of metaphor reminds us of the church bells that would have dominated this strict religious community and illustrates the fact that his broadcasting his shame in order to save his wife and neighbours represents a huge sacrifice on his part. This outcome of his struggle releases the tension in the audience, but only briefly as Miller begins to build it again with Abigail's 'stepping up to Danforth' and commanding, 'What look do you give me?…I'll not have such looks!'

Here the student has explored Miller's technique of using dramatic actions linked to the dialogue (the language of the play) to evoke tension in the audience and to underline the importance of a man's 'good name' in this community. They have shown that they understand how this tension

Grade _booster_

To change a word in an embedded quotation in order to make your sentence read fluently, you can use brackets around the word you need to change: Miller has Proctor tell Mary Warren that Abigail and he 'will slide together into [their] pit'. The actual quotation here would read 'will slide together into our pit'.

Grade _booster_

How to make quotation work for you:

1 Keep it short and sweet.

2 Make sure you embed it smoothly — it must make sense as an integral part of your whole sentence.

has been raised and how the use of metaphor in this section also helps to unpack Miller's thoughts and ideas to the audience.

AO3 and AO4

AO3 and AO4 are not tested for this play, but an important word is necessary regarding AO4.

AO4 tests your awareness and understanding of how knowledge of what was happening at the time a text was written may affect your understanding of it. For *The Crucible*, it will be impossible for you to show your understanding of the play (AO1) without making some reference to what was going on in Miller's society at the time he wrote it (AO4).

For example, there were no actual 'witch hunts' going on in 1950s America, but Senator McCarthy and his House Committee on Un-American Activities were actively 'hunting down' communists; their methods of conducting these searches and of trying those accused of communism are closely mirrored in Miller's play. Only when we know this does it become clear that the play is not just about witch hunts from a bygone age, but about modern 'witch hunts', also bred of fear of the unknown, with similarly disastrous effects in dividing a community and destroying the lives of individuals. In referring to the context of the play in this way, you will also be showing your understanding of it (AO1).

Review your learning

(Answers on p. 89)

1 What key words sum up AO1?

2 What key words sum up AO2?

3 Though AO4 is not tested directly, why might you still end up writing about context?

4 List four techniques that will boost your marks.

More interactive questions and answers online.

Tackling the assessments

- **How will you be assessed by the exam boards offering this text for study?**
- **How do you effectively plan and structure your responses?**
- **How do you effectively support your responses?**
- **How do you convince your assessor that you have developed an 'overview' of the play?**

Examination boards and tiers of entry

The Crucible features as a set text for AQA, and may well feature on your course for Edexcel, where the choice of texts is up to your teacher. **AQA** offers two levels of entry, **foundation or higher tier**, while for **Edexcel**, Unit 3, which will test your knowledge of Shakespeare and contemporary drama, is **untiered**.

For AQA, you need to be aware of how the two different levels of entry may affect the outcome of your award. At foundation level, the highest grade that you can attain is a C, while at the higher level, you may attain up to an A*, but cannot drop below a grade D or you will receive no award at all. The difference in the actual assessments is that at foundation level, questions include more guidance for students, usually in the form of bullet-pointed hints at what you might include in your answer. These hints also provide a useful framework for your essay. At the higher level, students need to plan their own essays without this sort of additional guidance. Your teacher will make the decision of which tier of entry to put you in for, depending upon how much assistance they think you might need, and they will reach this decision based upon your performance over the first year of your two-year course. You are at liberty to discuss this with them and most teachers would welcome this sign of interest.

Whichever of the above assessment paths applies to you, this chapter provides relevant detailed advice and exemplars of how to plan and write your essays in a way that will gain you maximum marks.

How will you be assessed by AQA?

Your knowledge and understanding of *The Crucible* is tested in **Unit 1** for this board (this applies to both 'routes' — A and B). This unit is entitled

Exploring Modern Texts and takes the shape of an external examination with two sections: section A: Modern Prose or Drama and section B: Exploring Cultures. Your questions on *The Crucible* will be found in **section A**. There will be a **choice of two**, of which you should **answer only one**. The examination lasts for 1½ hours and you are advised to spend **45 minutes** on each section. This is an **open book exam**, which means that you are allowed to take **un-annotated copies** of your text into the examination with you.

The chart below shows you the importance given to the different Assessment Objectives for English: the bold percentages indicate those relating to your study of *The Crucible*.

AQA Unit 1: Exploring Modern Texts	Section A: Modern Prose or Drama	Section B: Other Cultures	Overall GCSE
AO1	**10%**	5%	15%
AO2	**10%**	5%	15%
AO3	None	None	None
AO4	None	10%	10%
Overall GCSE:	**20%**	20%	40%

Note that you are not tested for AO3 or AO4 on this text, but without some knowledge of AO4 (the contexts in which the play was written), it is very unlikely that you will be able to show off your knowledge and understanding of the text (AO1) or the relevance of the ways in which Miller has wished to convey his points (AO2). (See the previous chapter for a full breakdown of these Assessment Objectives.)

Examples of AQA-style questions

Higher tier

Near the end of the play, John Proctor says to Elizabeth, 'I am no good man.' How does Miller present John Proctor? Is he a good man in your view?

Foundation tier

How does Miller present Abigail in *The Crucible*?
Write about:
- what Abigail is like
- the methods Miller uses to show what she is like

How will you be assessed by Edexcel?

For Edexcel, your assessment route will be through Unit 3 — and will be a 'controlled assessment' conducted not via an external examination, but supervised by your teachers, quite possibly in your own classroom during lesson time. The difference is that you will be allowed to prepare for your assessment beforehand, in the full knowledge of what your task will be. For the actual assessment itself, you will be given a total of **4 hours to complete two tasks**. These tasks will include an essay answer to **one question on Contemporary Drama** — for you, *The Crucible* — and **another on a play by Shakespeare**. Your Shakespeare task will be marked out of 30 and your task on Contemporary Drama out of 20. The uneven nature of the marks reflects the fact that you are required to compare your Shakespeare text to an adaptation of it — this might be a film version, or another written version (AO3) — whereas your question on *The Crucible* will focus purely on your knowledge and understanding (AO1) of this single text and the degree to which you understand how the ways in which Miller has conveyed his points have shaped your understanding of his meaning (AO2).

The following chart shows the relative importance given to the Assessment Objectives for this unit:

Edexcel Unit 3: Controlled Assessment: Shakespeare and Contemporary Drama	Shakespeare	Contemporary Drama: *The Crucible*	Overall
AO1	None	10%	10%
AO2	5%	None	5%
AO3	10%	None	10%
AO4	None	None	None
Overall	15%	10%	25%

Your teacher will be assessing this work, but an external moderator (working for the examination board) will also be called upon to agree the marks they have awarded. For your task on *The Crucible*, they will be looking for evidence that you have:

- responded to the play critically and imaginatively
- evaluated Miller's ways of expressing his meanings and achieving certain effects
- supported your ideas with well-chosen evidence from the play itself

The tasks will be set by the examination board and will offer a choice of four tasks on each of your texts. The choices for *The Crucible* will involve the following areas:

- character
- stagecraft
- themes
- relationships

You are expected to choose a task related to one of these areas and to develop and sustain an independent interpretation of the whole text in the light of this chosen area, supporting your overview with detailed references from the play.

By way of preparation for your tasks (before the 4 hours allocated to final written answers), you will be allowed to:

- work with other students and your teacher, which may include receiving their feedback on your ideas
- use the internet, watch television, film or live performances, and make notes in class

For the actual assessments (remember, you may not have as much as 2 hours for completion of your task on *The Crucible*, as this carries fewer marks than your Shakespeare response), you will be allowed access to:

- your notes
- a dictionary and thesaurus
- grammar and spell-checker programs

It is important that you understand that you will not be allowed to draft a response prior to the allocated time for the controlled assessment. Your notes must only include abbreviated or bullet-pointed ideas and not continuous phrases or paragraphs.

Examples of Edexcel-style tasks

EITHER
Characterisation
Explore the ways in which the dramatist introduces a key character to the audience.
Use examples from the text in your response.
OR
Stagecraft
With reference to two scenes or episodes, explore the dramatic devices used by the playwright to bring the drama to life.
Use examples from the text in your response.

OR

Theme

Explore the ways in which a key theme is presented in the drama.
Use examples from the text in your response.

OR

Relationships

Explore the ways in which a relationship between two characters is
introduced in the drama.
Use examples from the text in your response.

Planning and structuring your answers

General tips

First, here are some general tips to do with this genre. Remember, 'The
play's the thing...' (*Hamlet*, William Shakespeare). Whether being assessed
via the examination or controlled assessment method, you will need to
remember that for this part of your GCSE you are writing about drama,
which reaches the target audience in ways distinct from the other two
main genres you are studying: poetry and prose. The audience arrive at
an interpretation of the writer's possible meanings directly via their
physical senses of sight and sound, and even in a tactile way through
absorbing the atmosphere created by the actors in the auditorium in which
they are sitting.

> ### Grade *booster*
>
> If you are unable to see
> a live performance of
> *The Crucible*, make
> sure that you see a
> film version. The Daniel
> Day-Lewis version is
> excellent.

Pause for thought

Consider how it might feel to be part of a live audience watching some of the
highly charged scenes in this play: for example, the courtroom scenes where
Abigail and the others are making their wild accusations. Ask yourself how
you think that Miller has achieved the tension generated here. Is it something
to do with what the characters are saying, or with how they are saying it, or a
combination of both? Does the actual setting of the scene contribute to the
audience's response to these accusations?

Writing about characters

Whether in an examination or a controlled assessment, you cannot write
about a play without writing about the characters, as they are the primary
means through which a playwright shapes his or her meanings for the
audience. It is absolutely vital that you show your assessor your understanding that these characters are not real people, but constructs made up
by the writer as a means of developing his themes. Don't allow yourself to

ramble on about what the characters say and feel without referring to the author's possible point in making them say or feel these things.

Grade *focus*

For a C grade, statements about characters will mention the author's name, say what they have done with the character and begin to offer some explanation of the possible effect of this on the audience. For example:

> Miller has created Giles Corey as a man who knows about the law to make the point that this still didn't save people from death when the people being accused had to try to prove their own innocence against a charge that couldn't be proved in the first place.

For an A grade, the same rule applies, but use of language will be more sophisticated, and more detailed explanation will be offered, usually integrating a well-chosen quotation to help to strengthen and illustrate the point being made. For example:

> Miller has created Giles Corey as a man well versed in the law to reinforce the notion that even with all of his knowledge of the law, although this may save his land for his sons, it does not save his life. Miller seems to be highlighting that the nature of accusations of such designated crimes as witchcraft or communism is that they rely heavily on hearsay. This is reinforced when Proctor puts the question to Hale, 'Why do you never wonder if Parris be innocent, or Abigail? Is the accuser always holy now?'

Answering the question directly

This is not as obvious as it sounds. Whatever your task or question, you need to begin your response by addressing it head on. Your assessor does not want to hear what you 'intend' to do; they just want you to do it.

To make this clearer, take the following example of a typical AQA higher-tier question:

> Near the end of the play, John Proctor says to Elizabeth, 'I am no good man'. How does Miller present John Proctor? Is he a good man in your view?

This question is clearly asking for **your view**, so it is acceptable to begin with something like:
- In my view…
- I think that…
- It is clear to me that…
- It seems evident to me that…
- In my opinion…

Note that the question is double-barrelled:

1 How does Miller <u>present</u> John Proctor and

2 Is he a <u>good man</u> <u>in your view</u>?

The two are clearly related, however, so you can answer them in a 'oner', as follows:

In my view,**1** Miller intends us to see**2** Proctor as a good man at heart;**3** he achieves this by presenting him as more than one-dimensional.**4** We learn early on of his affair with Abigail, a young girl, whilst she was a servant in his household; hardly an act of goodness.**5** However, we also see his feelings of guilt and remorse and his sacrifice at the end of the play which show him to be at bottom, as Elizabeth says, 'a good man'.	**1** The student clearly signals that they are going to give their considered opinion. **2** This foregrounds the author to show that the student is aware that Proctor is not a real person, but a construct of the author. **3** The student qualifies 'as a good man' by adding 'at heart'. This signals to the assessor that he or she intends to argue that he doesn't always appear to behave in a good way. **4** The answer builds on this by showing that the student will develop the line that Proctor's character is complex rather than simple. **5** The student offers some support from the text to suggest the validity of the debate they are setting up in this opening.

This is a good opening which clearly addresses the demands of the question and opens up avenues of debate for the student to develop. The rest of the essay will seek to support this 'thesis' or central contention — here, that Miller presents Proctor as a good man 'at heart', though he is clearly a faulty human being. This opens the way to illustrate both Proctor's goodness and his faults, and through this analysis of character, to show how Miller's themes are revealed.

> **Grade booster**
>
> Notice in this opening how the student is signalling clearly to the assessor the argumentative path he or she is going to take.

> **Grade booster**
>
> Your opening should 'nail' the question. This is your 'thesis' and provides you with the hook upon which to hang the rest of your response. Every point you make after this should support and illustrate why your thesis is a valid one.

Now let's look at a typical controlled assessment task for **Edexcel**, and remember, these tasks are untiered.

> <u>Explore</u> the <u>ways in which</u> the <u>dramatist introduces</u> a <u>key character</u> to the audience. Use <u>examples from the text</u> in your response.

Every one of Edexcel's sample controlled assessment tasks features the word 'explore'. This is your key direction from the assessor regarding how they want you to approach your response. So, what does it mean?

> **Grade booster**
>
> Just as with the examination question, for a controlled assessment task, you need to highlight the key words to ensure you respond at the outset in a clearly focused way.

Explore means to look at a thing from different angles of approach and to analyse the possible effects of seeing it in these different ways. Look again at the question — here, you are asked to explore 'the ways in which' the writer has introduced a 'key' character. Note that there is an 's' on the end of 'way'. The task allows you to choose which character you want to 'explore' in this way, but the word 'key' narrows your choice. Think about what a 'key' does…it opens something up. So, what the assessor is saying is choose a character whom Miller uses to 'open something up' in his play. This 'something' will relate to his central ideas or themes. If you look again at the sections of this guide on character and theme, you will see that there are central, supporting and minor characters, all of whom are used by Miller to develop and illustrate his themes. However, you will have much more to say if you choose one of the central or supporting characters, whom Miller develops more fully.

Unlike the AQA examination question, this is a task, but it still needs to be addressed head-on. The same approach of flagging up the important words in the task will help you to focus your response throughout the body of your essay. You might begin this task in the following way:

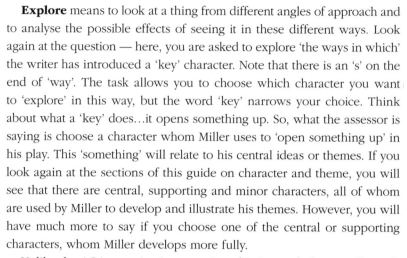

1 This foregrounds the author.

2 This opens up an avenue for talking about these various different techniques.

3 The student shows the assessor that they know they have to focus on the 'introduction' of the character, not how the character is 'developed' later in the play or how the character 'changes', for instance — other directive words that might have been chosen.

4 Here the student signals which 'key' character they have chosen.

5 This begins the central point in general terms.

6 The student then starts to open this out with another aspect that they will develop further in the body of the response.

7 Again, this sets up a point about Miller's possible purpose for this character that will allow the student to show how Miller uses Proctor to help him convey his themes to the audience.

Miller**1** uses a variety of interesting techniques**2** to introduce**3** the key character of John Proctor**4** to the audience.

It is critical, for example, that we, the audience, don't see Proctor until we have first understood much about the belief systems, superstitions and politics of this community.**5** In this way, when Proctor does appear, the ways that the other characters respond to him**6** make clear that Miller is going to use him as a sort of catalyst in the action of the play.**7**

Developing and supporting your answer

The central body of the response will need to develop the point or points you have laid down in your opening. For example, having mentioned in general terms that Miller introduces Proctor as 'a catalyst' (something that sets off a reaction or series of reactions) in the action of the play, you now need to show in detail how he does this.

You need to take the assessor into the play now and point out exactly which parts of it gave you the idea you have just proposed.

There is a neat little formula or framework that you can use in order to make each successive point that will support your opening thesis. It is called PEE and stands for the following:

Point — that is, make a point.

Evidence — use a reference to the play/some quotation to illustrate your point.

Explain — the effect of this upon the audience.

Using PEE

Taking the above question as an example, you could continue in this way with your first illustration of your thesis.

The first reaction to John Proctor's entrance**1** is that 'upon seeing him, Mary Warren leaps in fright',**2** revealing to the audience that he is a character of some strength who commands respect and even fear.**3**

1 Point — picks up the idea of his being used as a catalyst.

2 Evidence — builds in a quotation to show what has shaped this idea.

3 Explanation — of the effect of this upon the audience; what it reveals about the character.

Think of this process of PEE as a way of building the blocks of your argument.

For a higher grade, you might continue with the following 'link' phrases that lead into another reference to the play:

- Miller further illustrates this point by…
- This idea is reinforced when…
- The writer consolidates this view of Proctor through…
- The audience's impression of Proctor as…is further strengthened by…

Any of these introductions to your second PEE block will lead you into your next piece of quotation, which you can then follow up with your explanation of its effect on the audience. So, for example, you might continue:

Miller strengthens this initial impression**1** when we read, in his long direction that follows Mary Warren's reaction, that he is 'a farmer in his mid-thirties' with 'a sharp and biting way with hypocrites' and that 'in Proctor's presence a fool felt his foolishness — and a Proctor is always marked for calumny therefore.'**2** This signals clearly to the audience that John Proctor represents a well-known human type; one that stands his ground and makes his feelings of contempt for others clear, when he feels this to be justified.**3**

Grade *booster*

Should you wish to gain a grade higher than a C, you need to develop the point you have made before moving on to another point, by adding another few PEE 'blocks' to show how Miller has further strengthened this idea for you.

1 Point — fluently linked to the one just made.

2 Evidence — builds in a quotation to support and illustrate.

3 Explanation — explores the possible effect of this on the audience.

4 This develops the explanation further with reference to the key words of the task: in other words, introduction of the character is signalled with the words 'from the start' and followed up by the beginnings of an exploration of how Miller is going to use Proctor to illustrate his general theme of how and why 'witch hunts' can occur in a community.

> It is obvious then from the start, that Proctor is going to be a man with enemies in this community that we have already been shown is deeply divided by personal agendas, made clear from the previous interactions between Parris and Putnam.**4**

Grade *booster*

A winning conclusion will always develop a final point that clearly relates to what you have stated in your introduction and will really convince your assessor that your thesis is an intelligent, valid and interesting one.

Concluding your essay or task

Again, this is not rocket science. All you need to do is save a really good point that clinches (gives excellent support for) your thesis, and develop it in your conclusion using the same method of PEE.

First, look again at the earlier exemplar opening for the AQA sample higher-tier question:

> Near the end of the play, John Proctor says to Elizabeth, 'I am no good man'. <u>How</u> does <u>Miller present John Proctor</u>? Is he a <u>good man</u> in <u>your view</u>?

> In my view, Miller intends us to see Proctor as a good man at heart; he achieves this by presenting him as more than one-dimensional. We learn early on of his affair with Abigail, a young girl, whilst she was a servant in his household; hardly an act of goodness. However, we also see his feelings of guilt and remorse and his sacrifice at the end of the play which show him to be at bottom, as Elizabeth says, 'a good man'.

Having begun in this way and then developed your central thesis (idea) throughout, using the PEE building block method, you might conclude with the following point, 'saved' up to clinch the argument you've been illustrating throughout your answer:

1 The answer highlights the focus of the question.

2 A hint is given of how this will be developed in the concluding point.

3 This foregrounds the author at work and his possible intentions.

4 Quotations are embedded smoothly to illustrate the point.

> What Miller seems to be suggesting about Proctor is that he represents a man who earnestly wishes to be good,**1** whose passionate nature has led him astray in his affair with Abigail and who is then caught up through this personal weakness, in social circumstances beyond his control.**2** In having Proctor seek to protect his wife and neighbours from the vindictiveness of his jilted mistress, Miller mirrors the way that personal agendas can spill over into the community and become widely destructive; Abigail's vindictiveness has far-reaching effects.**3** When Elizabeth answers 'No, sir' to Danforth's question, 'Is your husband a lecher!', only to find that John had already admitted his fault, sacrificing his good name in order to save his wife and neighbours, Miller has Hale cry out, 'I beg you, stop now before another is condemned…private vengeance is working through this testimony!' **4** It seems clear through this that Miller's primary wish is that his audience is not too pre-occupied with the question of a single character's

goodness; there are many less ambiguously 'good' characters in the play such as Goody Nurse.**5** What he may be wishing his audience to reflect upon is that these characters, whose situation mirrors the McCarthyism of 1950s America, reflect a world where regardless of one's level of goodness, when authority puts a stamp of approval on persecution, an entire community can become embroiled in 'private vengeance' masquerading as public concern.**6** In this he creates a perfect allegory of the way in which McCarthy's zeal in seeking out communists provided individuals with the perfect opportunity to play out their private vengeances in the public arena and actually be congratulated by the government in doing so.**7**

This is typical of the sort of conclusion that a student working at A* level might produce.

5 This explains the effect of this bit of quoted dialogue upon the audience with reference to the focus of the question, expanding and developing the idea.

6 The point is developed further, showing an overview of what Miller might have been trying to achieve through the writing of the play.

7 The piece ends with a clincher in saying something about the form of the play — an allegory — and the effect of this in contextual terms.

Grade *focus*

To achieve a grade C, your answers will need to focus clearly on the question or task throughout. You will need to state your thesis clearly (in your introduction), follow the PEE method of illustrating and supporting this thesis, and write a clear and well-focused conclusion that does more than simply summarise the points you've already made. In order to gain a higher grade, you will need to improve the quality of your analysis of the play by developing each of these elements further, looking more deeply into what the playwright might have been trying to convey to his audiences and the specific ways in which he has tried to do this. An A* will be awarded to responses that argue points not only clearly but with sophistication and that refers very closely, with appropriate support, to the play itself.

Review your learning

(Answers on p. 89)

1. If following Edexcel, what method will your assessment follow and which Assessment Objectives will you be tested on?
2. As question 1, but for AQA.
3. Regardless of which method is followed, what are the three vital structural elements of your response?
4. Do you need to talk about context in your response?

More interactive questions and answers online.

Sample essays

AQA

It must be stressed that the examples that follow are partial, particularly the middle sections of responses. However, it is the techniques that are being used that should be your primary focus here, just as with examples already given in the previous two chapters.

All of the sample essays in this guide illustrate essay-writing skills that are relevant, regardless of which exam board you are studying with. You simply need to note that the questions or tasks are framed slightly differently and that Edexcel assesses AO1 only for this unit, while AQA will be assessing AO1 and AO2.

AQA higher tier

Theme-based question

How does Miller present ideas about beliefs in *The Crucible*?

A*-grade answer

1 This opening clearly foregrounds the author and is completely 'nailed' to the focus of the task; it sets up clearly the thesis that the student is going to pursue: the idea that beliefs can destroy people's lives. Note that the key word, 'beliefs', does not just mean religious beliefs, but could refer to other sorts of belief (e.g. in witchcraft, in the absolute sanctity of a courtroom, in the idea that the law is above everything, etc.)

2 Here the student is dealing extremely ably and, again, directly with the part of the task that requires analysis of *the ways* Miller presents his idea. This is about his dramatic techniques — the student focuses the assessor on an exploration of how Miller is working on the visual and auditory senses of his audience.

3 A well-integrated quotation is given to illustrate the point and show that it is well grounded in the text.

Beginning

Miller presents the idea of beliefs in general, not just religious beliefs, being powerful enough to utterly destroy a person's life right from the moment the curtain is raised on the action of the play.**1** Even before dialogue is introduced, Miller appeals to the visual and auditory senses of his audience by presenting**2** a man 'kneeling…in prayer', by the side of his sick daughter's bed, 'with a sense of confusion…about him. He mumbles, then seems about to weep; then he weeps, then prays again.'**3** This shows us at once that his belief in God does not seem to bring him any peace in the face of calamity. He seems at this stage to be overcome with grief about the illness of his child, but this only increases the audience's reaction of surprise and interest when it becomes clear that his disturbance is more on account of the superstitious beliefs of his neighbours that 'unnatural cause' may be behind Betty's illness.**4** So terrified is he of what the community may do to him should this turn out to be their judgement, that he has, ironically as it is later revealed, 'sent for Reverend Hale', a man believed to be an expert in seeking out witchcraft, who will 'put out all thought of unnatural causes' in this case.**5**

4 An exploration is offered of what Miller might be trying to convey to the audience through this. Note how a short snippet of further quotation has been smoothly embedded to help the student to make this point.

5 Further exploration and illustration of the same idea. Again, quotation has been skilfully embedded to support and illustrate the thesis.

This opening has all the elements of an A* answer. It is well focused, fluent and well illustrated, and already shows the assessor clearly that the student is aware that he or she is writing about a play, rather than a novel or a piece of poetry.

Middle

One way in which**1** Miller signals to the audience that beliefs can be fabricated to suit an individual's personal agenda and that there is no way of refuting them**2** is through his use of Hale, Ann Putnam, Tituba and Abigail in Act One.**3** At the end of Act One, we see that Abigail, who we've already been told has 'an endless capacity for dissembling', has worked out that Tituba's acquiescence with Ann Putnam's suggestion of women who have been 'with the Devil' is a way of clearing her own name. Miller has Abigail rise, 'staring as though inspired' and crying out, 'I want to open myself!'**4** The directions further state that the other characters on stage 'turn to her, startled' and that she 'is enraptured, as though in a pearly light'. The effect of this upon the audience, who have seen more than the other characters on stage, for example Abigail's slapping Betty when her Uncle Parris is out of the room and her forthright lust for John Proctor, will be one of horror as they realise that she is both able and prepared to condemn innocent people to death, to clear herself. Through Hale's exclamation, 'Glory to God! It is broken, they are free!', it is clear that Miller wishes his audience to be see how readily even a well-intentioned individual like Hale has the potential to believe what they want to believe.**5**

1 This is a useful lead-in phrase.

2 This point is clearly linked to the focus of the question — how Miller presents ideas about beliefs.

3 'How' is addressed here — use of characterisation.

4 Quotation is used to illustrate the point and explanation is given of the effects of this reference upon the audience.

5 Further detailed references and explanation are given of possible meanings and effects upon the audience. Again, the student is clearly focused upon the task, and this is flagged up to the assessor by use of the word 'believe' at the end of the paragraph.

The use of PEE is fluent, detailed and sophisticated, as would be expected of a response at this level.

Conclusion

Just as with the McCarthyism and the communist 'witch-hunts' of his own day, Miller shows us in this play the 'panic' that began to 'set in' when some members of the community 'began to turn toward greater individual freedom' (Overture, Act One).**1** The accounts of the girls dancing naked at the beginning of the play seems representative of this desire for greater individual freedom from a strict religious order that saw pleasure as sinful.**2** Their choice of the woods is surely symbolic of what Miller terms the 'virgin forest',

1 A final point related to the focus of the question — Miller's presentation of ideas on beliefs. The student uses quotation from Miller's overture to illustrate the point.

2 The student highlights a way the idea is presented through off-stage action of characters.

seen by most inhabitants of Salem as 'the Devil's last preserve' (Overture, Act One). **3** Likewise, John Proctor's non-attendance at church is flung in his face early on in Act One by Thomas Putnam, and Cheever in Act Three tells Danforth, 'he plough on Sunday, sir', and we see that this information puts Proctor in an extremely vulnerable position from Danforth's shocked, 'Plough on Sunday!' Both are seen as presenting a danger to the 'New Jerusalem' and its belief systems.**4** In the readiness of the court to believe the accusations of those with individual interests such as Abigail and Thomas Putnam, Miller highlights how this protectionist attitude towards one set of beliefs was instrumental in tearing apart the community it was meant to hold together. It lays a community open to 'crazy children…jangling the keys of the kingdom, and common vengeance writ[ing] the law!' These metaphors remind us graphically of how ideas of freedom and justice are coupled with the question that Miller has John Proctor put to Hale, 'Is the accuser always holy now?'**5** This is surely a question Miller wished the American populace to ask themselves in the face of lives being destroyed by the individually motivated accusations made against people reported to McCarthy's Committee. These 'witch-hunts' too were carried out in the name of an utter belief in the rightness of one way of life over all others.**6**

This conclusion convincingly suggests a strong personal engagement with the play and excellent knowledge and understanding of what may have been Miller's intentions in writing it, but it stays within the bounds of the specific task focus. It is this sense of a developing overview that would gain the student an A* as opposed to simply a grade A.

AQA foundation tier

Character-based question

How do you respond to Danforth in *The Crucible*?
Write about:
- what you think about what he does and says
- the methods Miller uses to present him

C-grade answer

Beginning

I don't like Danforth and I don't think Miller wants us to like him.**1** From his first being seen on stage in Act Three he seems arrogant and full of himself,**2** telling Giles Corey he is disrupting the court when he is trying to stand up for his wife. 'Disrespect indeed! It is disruption, Mister. This is the highest court of the supreme government of this province, do you know it?'**3** He refuses to listen to Giles. 'Then let him submit his evidence in proper affidavit.' Danforth also refuses to listen to Nurse and seems more concerned with his own importance, asking him, 'Do you know who I am, sir?'**4** He also appears to be proud of the number of people he has condemned to hang 'and seventy-two condemned to hang'.**5** All of this makes him an unlikeable character from the start.

3 Quotation is offered but is put into the sentence without regard to grammatical correctness, so that the fluency of the argument is disrupted. The quotation is also a little longer than it needs to be to illustrate the point.

4 The student builds upon his or her response to Danforth here with a further illustration. This could have been made far more detailed with closer reference to why Nurse was there and the evidence he brought with him.

5 A further piece of evidence is given of Danforth's unpleasant nature. It is well chosen, but poorly integrated again.

Grade *booster*

Remember to use formal language, not colloquialisms such as 'full of himself'. Here the expression 'self-absorbed' or 'self-centred' would be far more appropriate and gain higher marks.

The student does show clear knowledge and understanding of how Miller has presented Danforth as an unsympathetic (unlikeable) character, though in fairly straightforward and simplistic terms. Engagement with the text is evident, and with more detailed reference to the play, closer attention to use of language and a more fluent integration of quotation, this could have been a much better opening.

Conclusion

Finally, the most unlikeable thing about Danforth is that Miller shows him to care more about his own reputation than about killing people who may not even be guilty. 'I cannot pardon these when twelve are already hanged for the same crime. It is not just.' He doesn't ask himself whether or not he might have been mistaken in the twelve that have already died but wishes to justify his actions by hanging more people.**1** He even says 'postponement now speaks a floundering on my part; reprieve or pardon must cast doubt upon the guilt of them that died till now.' This shows that safeguarding his own reputation is more important to him than saving lives. He won't accept that he may have been wrong or do anything that might suggest he even thinks this.**2** When Hale asks Danforth to let Proctor go home and get a lawyer to argue his case, Danforth is patronising 'Now look you, Mr Hale —' and 'you surely do not doubt my justice'.**3** This final statement might make the audience think that he

1 The student has saved a good point to finish on and signposts the conclusion clearly with the word 'Finally'. PEE is used effectively here.

2 A little more detail in the way of further quotation helps to develop this point more convincingly, and the explanation is clear, convincing and fairly succinct, with a good use of language.

3 More good use of language is evident here in the use of 'patronising', although the quotation, while appropriate, is not smoothly embedded.

4 This is an insightful point, showing a good level of engagement with Miller's characterisation and an awareness of audience reaction.

5 Most examiners would probably be open to a remark like this right at the end of a question that has asked for your personal opinion of, or response to, a character, but be careful not to make many statements like this and make sure that if you do, they are fully supported by your more serious analysis of the question, as is the case here.

doesn't really believe that he is the voice of God as he claims later as he talks about 'his' justice here and not God's.**4** He's not a man that you would want to buy a used car from!**5**

This is quite a strong conclusion that is only held back from a B grade by a lack of fluency, the need for a clearer foregrounding of the author and a slightly clumsy use of quotation in places.

Edexcel

Untiered

Relationships-based controlled assessment task

> Explore the ways in which a relationship between two characters is introduced in the drama.
> Use examples from the text in your response.

Focus = the relationship between Proctor and Abigail.

C-grade answer

1 The student clearly signals the relationship he or she is going to focus on and states clearly where it is first introduced.

2 This shows an implicit awareness of the effect of structuring of the play on audience response: that is, the effect of Miller's having Proctor and Abigail left alone in Betty's bedroom.

3 A relevant quotation (not very well integrated) is used to illustrate how Miller's use of dialogue gives the audience further clues regarding the nature of their relationship.

4 This reveals an understanding of how this dialogue, linked to the structuring of the scenes, informs the audience's response, though again, this is implicit rather than explicit.

5 This is the most fluent section of the introduction. Another technique is highlighted (body language) and quotation is embedded smoothly to support the stated effect upon the audience.

Beginning

The relationship between Proctor and Abigail is introduced in Act One.**1** When Abigail and John Proctor are left alone in Betty's bedroom the audience would guess that something is going on between them.**2** Abigail talks to him in a personal way 'Gah! I'd almost forgot how strong you are, John Proctor!' and when she tells him about their dancing in the woods, he smiles at her and tells her 'Ah, you're wicked yet, aren't y'!' and 'You'll be clapped in the stocks before you're twenty.'**3** This shows us that they have had a relationship that has been hidden from the rest of the community as they don't talk to each other like this when the others are in the room.**4** The audience might guess from Abigail's body language that she is interested in John Proctor in a sexual way when Miller says that she moves 'closer' to him 'feverishly looking into his eyes.'**5**

This is a typical C-grade opening; it is clear, well focused on the task and offers relevant supporting material. For a B or an A, more understanding of the writer at work is needed. This could be signalled to the assessor through a foregrounding of the writer's name, more explanation of the possible intentions of the writer and how he achieves desired effects, and a smoother use of quotation, as in point 5 above.

Now look at the A*-grade opening below, for the same task.

A*-grade answer

Beginning

In order to make clear the illicit and dangerous nature of the relationship between Abigail and Proctor, Miller cleverly structures his opening scenes so that his audience find out something about Abigail before they see them together.**1** It is revealed that she is two faced and the leader of a group of girls in the village, when she is left alone with Betty and 'smashes her across the face' immediately after appearing so meek and submissive in front of her uncle.**2** The use of the word 'smashes' here is particularly important as it denotes the passionate and potentially violent nature of Abigail and ensures that the audience see her as someone who likes to have her own way and doesn't care who she hurts to gain it.**3** Miller's audience will be left in no doubt then that just as he states in his directions, Abigail is a young woman not only 'strikingly beautiful' which would give her some power in a puritan community where beauty was a rare thing, but with 'an endless capacity for dissembling'.**4** This makes her a potentially dangerous individual and Miller plays on the fact that the audience see far more than the other characters on stage. Proctor does not witness her violence against the younger girls, but the audience do.**5**

1 The essay makes very clear here an understanding of the nature of the relationship between Abigail and Proctor, and sets out explicitly one of the ways in which this is introduced in the opening scenes, not forgetting to foreground the author.

2 This develops an important insight that Miller gives us into Abigail's nature and embeds highly relevant quotation smoothly to illustrate the point.

3 A detailed exploration is made of the effect of this word and how the actress playing the part would be revealed as a result.

4 A more detailed analysis is offered of the audience's impression of Abigail, which will inform our understanding of the relationship between her and Proctor.

5 This shows more explicit analysis of a 'way in which' their relationship is introduced: that is, superior audience awareness.

Grade *booster*

Remember, the rules for using quotation:
- little and often
- smoothly embedded

This will make your arguments more succinct, fluent and persuasive.

Middle

When Proctor enters, Miller shows the audience immediately her attraction to him and his to her, in their body language. She 'has stood on tiptoe, absorbing his presence, wide-eyed' and when they speak after the other characters have

6 Like the C-grade opening, body language is picked up on, but here a more detailed analysis with a smoother use of quotation makes the point far more explicitly.

exited, about the cause of Betty's illness, he looks at Abigail with 'the faintest suggestion of a knowing smile on his face', all of which reveals to the audience that they have a secret knowledge of one another that they keep hidden when others are in the room.**6**

The battle of wills between these two surrounding their illicit relationship is further illustrated to us when…

A solid A* opening leads the way into an essay that can elaborate on the highly charged interplay between these two characters that follows in this scene. Remember the focus of the task — here it is all about how the relationship is *introduced*.

1 The student sums up the nature of their relationship as introduced by Miller, and a very explicit awareness of audience is evident here. A skilfully embedded piece of quotation opens the way for the next PEE block.

2 The point is elaborated with more skilful use of quotation.

3 Detailed explanatory analysis is given of the point that Miller is making through this relationship and of its role within the play as a whole.

4 This is a succinct summing up of the part that the relationship plays in conveying one of Miller's central themes, linked to the context of his own time, showing an overview of the play.

Conclusion

The relationship between these two characters is introduced primarily then as a destructive one and Miller makes this starkly apparent to his audience by the way that Abigail swings from one highly charged emotion to another when John Proctor tells her their affair is 'done with'.**1** First she 'can't believe it', then she tries 'softening' and 'weeping' before she 'clutches him desperately' and then responds to his 'gently pressing her from him' with 'a flash of anger'.**2** It is this flash of anger and the following expression of 'bitter anger' combined with the audience's previous knowledge of Abigail's capacity for manipulation and violence, that would make clear to anyone watching the play how dangerous Abigail is to John Proctor. She is the classic woman scorned in love and she will not take it lightly. Through this introduction of their relationship the audience are shown that it is going to be a key relationship in the play that will be a catalyst for much of the subsequent action of the play.**3** It is private 'vengeance' that is at the root of the accusations of witchcraft, just as so many accusations of communism were motivated by private grudges in Miller's own society.**4**

(See also examples of other Edexcel controlled assessment responses in the previous chapter.)

Review your learning

(Answers on p. 90)
1. What do you need to do in the opening of your response?
2. How do you convince the assessor that you are aware that this is a play?
3. What technique will help you to ensure that the assessor sees you are aware of the writer at work?
4. What do you need to do in your conclusion to ensure that you clinch your argument?

More interactive questions and answers online.

Answers

Answers to *Review your learning* questions.

Context (p. 12)

1 The American government feared that communist sympathisers would spread their political ideas among other American citizens, and plot to do harm to their country. The puritan authorities in Salem feared that witches in their community would draw more people into witchcraft and attack other God-fearing citizens.
2 They were eager to condemn other people as witches in order to settle old scores or purchase land that would be forfeit to the authorities if the landowners were condemned as witches and executed.

   They did not want to be seen to stand up against the authorities, who believed their community was under attack from witchcraft.
3 Miller wanted to show his audiences the dangers of supporting attacks by authority on innocent people.
4 It created a society where people lived together in unity against hardships they faced in the colony: the threat of Native American Indian attacks and the immensely hard work involved in creating and maintaining farms that were their only source of food.

Plot and structure (p. 35)

1 Parris — self interested, materialistic, fearful.
   Abigail — wilful, passionate, angry.
   Ann Putnam — bitter, keen to find guilt where none exists.
   Thomas Putnam — greedy.
   Hale — proud, keen to impress people with his knowledge of witchcraft.
2 Each of them has had his wife arrested on suspicion of witchcraft.

   Giles Corey feels completely innocent of any involvement in his wife's arrest; Francis Nurse feels guilt that he may have suggested something (his wife's reading a book) that contributed to the situation, while John Proctor knows not only that his wife is innocent, but that the whole witch hunt is based on lies.
3 Throughout his questioning of various people, especially John Proctor, through Act Three, Danforth is given stage and line directions by Miller suggesting that he is listening intently, thinking deeply and actively

considering whether the claims made by Proctor against the trials are in fact true. In the end, however, Danforth is committed to the law.

4 Parris has lost his savings; Hale has recognised the evil he colluded with in the trials.

Characterisation (p. 50)

1 It influences and shapes the character of John Proctor, provides a potential motive for Abigail accusing Elizabeth Proctor of witchcraft, and creates the dilemma facing John of having to confess his secret affair to the court in order to prove how he knows that the claims of witchcraft being made are false.

2 As their situations become desperate — Elizabeth is in jail and then John is also arrested and faces death — they reveal their deep love for one another. Elizabeth becomes able to forgive her husband his sexual affair with Abigail.

3 Giles Corey is a man of honour and his word, yet he has an argumentative and acquisitive side that causes him to engage in endless disputes with his neighbours.

Hale is — at the start of the play — committed to bringing his 'specialised knowledge' of witches to the witch trials, yet by the end of the play he has seen the damage he has helped cause, recognised the trials as based on lies, is racked with guilt and wishes to make amends.

4 She has a reputation for honesty, yet she is a loyal wife and so Danforth suspects that she would try and 'read' any signs Proctor might try to give her.

Themes (p. 59)

1 Symbols of authority:
- Parris has spiritual authority over the community because he is their appointed church leader.
- Hale has 'special knowledge' of witchcraft to lead the investigations.
- Danforth and Hathorne have legal authority as judges.

Those who stand up to authority:
- John Proctor
- Rebecca Nurse
- Giles Corey
- Francis Nurse

2 They are highly dramatic and theatrical moments that bring noise, energy and tension to the closing moments of two acts, driving the pace of the story forward.

These moments also show how absurd the girls' hysterical accusations are to our eyes, though they are utterly believed by the adults in the Salem courtroom. Miller wants us to see how gullible and ready to be deceived these people were.

3 Parris briefly gains power as the community's spiritual leader in a time of crisis.

Hale enjoys the power of having special and appropriate knowledge to support the witch hunts.

Abigail and all the girls enjoy the high status of being crucial to the court's work.

Cheever gains some status by becoming an official of the court.

4 Parris — to increase his spiritual authority.

The Putnams — to buy land forfeited to the court by accused people.

Abigail (and the girls) — to deflect possible criticism of their dancing in the woods and playing at raising spirits.

Tituba — to save her life by becoming the first person to confess to witchcraft.

Style (p. 63)

1 Miller is trying to convey the sense of a community where individuality is frowned upon.
2 You will find lots of the first and very little of the second. There is far more anger and rhetoric in this play than love or poetry.
3 The speeches of many characters are infused with anger and images of fire and punishment, of guilt and sin, that is resonant of the more violent and graphic passages of the Old Testament of the Bible.

Assessment Objectives and skills (p. 68)

1 Own writing; knowledge and understanding.
2 Language; form; structure.
3 Because if you aren't aware of what was going on in Miller's society at the time, you will miss entirely the message of this play, which is what you are being tested upon for AO1.
4 Foreground the author; use PEE; quote little and often; don't forget to use quotation marks.

Tackling the assessments (p. 79)

1 Internal controlled assessment; AO1 only (your knowledge and understanding of the play and the clarity of your own expression).

2 External examination; AOs 1 and 2 (as above, and the ways in which the writer has put these ideas across to you, i.e. their literary techniques or methods).

3 An introduction, which sets out your thesis (the argument you intend to develop); the body of your essay, where you use the building block PEE method to back up and illustrate your thesis; and your conclusion, for which you save up a really good point that fully supports your thesis, adding a little something more if you are aiming for an A*.

4 You are not being tested on AO4, but if you are to show your understanding of the play (AO1), you really cannot avoid bringing up the social and literary contexts in which it was written (see, for example, the sample conclusion to the AQA specimen question in this section).

Sample essays (p. 86)

1 Focus clearly on the key words of the task and answer the question or address the task squarely and firmly. This is where you effectively answer the question, and the rest of your essay is there to prove that your answer is a valid one.

2 Write about the *effects* that different authorial techniques have upon the *audience*. Especially remember to analyse the effects of the visual (body language) and audio (the way the dialogue is delivered as well as what the characters say). Playwrights work upon the senses of their audience to help them to convey their thoughts and ideas.

3 Foreground the writer — mention Miller's name in saying what he is trying to achieve through any of the many techniques that he uses.

4 You need to save a really good point for your conclusion and use it to clinch your thesis (your opening statement/answer to the question).

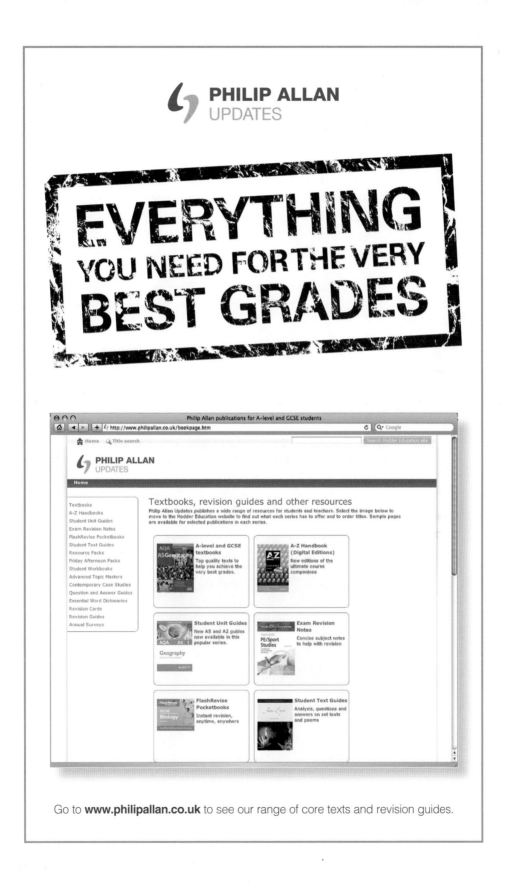